Teach Me

AB MONNETTE

First edition

Cover art by Natchlee Joseph

 Formatted with Vellum

To my dear sister,
Whom I didn't realize shared Aisha's age until the very last minute.
... I can't believe you're turning eighteen this year.

Content Warning

Suicidal ideation
Medical trauma
Psychological distress
Alcohol consumption
Morally gray characters
Use of Drugs and Alcohol
Mention of Death

Author's Note

Dear Readers,

Thank you for choosing to read *"Teach Me".* If you haven't read "Touch me", I highly recommend that you go back and read that first, or you'll be left in confusion.

I'm still doing this publishing thing solo (#shoutoutindieauthors), but I have more (ethical) resources that make it a bit easier, yay!!

At first, I wasn't going to write about Aisha's parents, but my Wattpad audience (hii y'all) encouraged it.

Before you start, I want to give a few warnings. Feel free to skip if you want zero spoilers.

First, James doesn't have a textbook diagnosis. If you try to compare his issues (and any issues brought up) to a real-life diagnosis, you will get confused.

I'm a perfectionist and a Psychology student. If I actually focused on accuracy, this book would never get published. So to bypass that, I want you all to know one thing (this applies to all my books): every medical condition mentioned, no matter how similar to real life... is made up and/or exaggerated. Even if the names are the same.

After all, this is a romance book, not a medical book.

(This also applies to geography, politics, timelines, technology, etc., etc.)

Second, James MAY NOT be your favorite book boyfriend (but if you've already read Touch Me, you know this). He has his flaws, and they won't be fixed by love. To be honest... it gets a bit worse in some areas.

Lastly, you will be left with answers. Some things will not be vague. You might even say to yourself, "I wonder what happened to this." Trust me, everything will be tied up in book 3. This book, though book 2, is more of a prequel than a sequel.

With all that being said, I hope you all enjoy this read. From dealing with grief, seasonal depression, to impostor syndrome that led to me deleting half of the book the day before publishing, this was a journey to write.

I thank you all for your understanding and patience.

With all my Love,

A.B Monnette

Prologue

JAMES

2027

Knock. Knock.

"Come in,"

The door to my office opens slowly.

I watch my wife walk with two glasses of whiskey in her hand. She gives me a small smile, sitting on my lap without an invitation.

Not that she needed one.

Taking the whiskey from her hand, I take a sip and kiss her on the lip. Her presence brings me peace.

I shrug, eyes back to the security camera at Aisha's prom. She and that boyfriend of hers were currently dancing to a slow song.

"I don't like him," I mutter, glaring at the boy through the screen.

"Liar," My wife teases, laying her head on my chest. "Do I need to ask you about the sudden death of that officer who arrested him?"

"Heart attack."

"Or why was it so easy to change his name on his birth certificate and seal off his record?"

"I don't know what you're talking about."

She laughs, "Deny all you want, but I know you like that boy. If you didn't, he and Aisha wouldn't be together, no matter how much she fought you on that."

"I think you're wrong, Daisy,"

She cocks a brow at my words. I don't often tell her she's wrong.

"The way our little princess acted when he was in the hospital, I wouldn't be surprised if she left us for him. She loves him."

She stays silent for a bit before nodding, "Like father, like daughter."

With that, we stay quiet, me nursing my whiskey, while Daisy lies on me, both of us watching our daughter enjoying her last few days of high school. As my wife falls asleep on me, and the dance ends, I click on another file on the computer, and a slideshow of pictures starts.

I let my mind wander to the past, when a certain klutz spilled coffee on me the day of her interview. That same klutz who taught me how to feel.

DESIREE

2000

Alright. You got this.

I take a deep breath and repeat the mantra over and over again, grasping my shaking hands and massaging them.

It's just a simple job interview, that's all.

I spare myself another glance in the mirror, making sure not one hair is out of place, and that my clothes have no stains or wrinkles.

Perfect.

I walk out of my room, almost colliding with my sister, Lauren, who was standing in front of the doorway.

"May I help you?"

She ignores my question, giving me a once-over, "Why are you dressed so nice? Aren't you just applying to be a janitor or something?"

I give her a tight smile, walking past her, "Dress for your dream job is what they always say?"

"That only applies to people with college degrees and a future."

Ignoring the sting, I don't entertain her answer. Instead, I make my way to the kitchen down the hall to eat the food I prepared myself this morning.

The same food being eaten by my mother and father.....

My dad was the first to see me, and a look of shame quickly flashed on his face before it disappeared. "Oh, we thought you left?"

"Why the get up? It's just a janitorial job."

I couldn't help but roll my eyes at my mom's comment; she and my sister were the same people.

Inconsiderate. Rude. Bit-.

"I'm leaving now, might spend the night with JJ tonight."

My mom snorts at that. She hates it when I bring up my boyfriend or when I spend the night with him. I'm sure she and my sister are betting on how long it'll take for me to get pregnant.

Little do they know, I have never slept with JJ. We both decided to wait till marriage, his idea, not mine.

"What about breakfast?" She calls out as I make my way out the door.

You're eating it.

"I'll pass by a coffee shop or something."

I was running late for my interview.

The line at the coffee shop was unfairly long, my bus broke down, and I had to walk two blocks to reach a transfer stop.

Even so, I was only five minutes late. Which isn't much, but from what I've read about this company, they are strict. Although they legally have to give a 15-minute grace period, they basically throw away any latecomers' resumes.

I know I'm just applying for a custodian job, but deep down, I can feel that the hiring agent is picky, no matter what position they're interviewing for.

Please, let me get this job. I know it's not much, but it's enough to get me away from that fucking corner store. The pay and benefits are good, and near a community college. I don't know what I would be learning, but that's a problem for future me. So please, ope-

"Oof," My prayers were cut short when I bumped into someone outside the building. I watch in horror as my white blouse gets soaked by the coffee that was in my hand.

Looking up, my eyes widen in horror when I see the man in front of me suffering a worse fate than I, "I am sooooo sorry, I wasn't looking and was in a rush because I have this intervi-"

He cuts my words short by walking away, not sparing a single glance my way.

This day can't get any worse.

Two

DESIREE

2000

I stand corrected.

The day did get worse.

I couldn't salvage my shirt in the company bathroom; all I ended up doing was spreading the stain. By the time I made it to the hiring manager's office, I looked like a hot mess, and I could tell by the way his eyes narrowed at me that I wasn't getting the job.

As I answered his questions, the reflection in his glasses showed me that.

He was playing fucking solitaire.

"Mr. Lance?"

No answer.

Taking the hint, I start to gather my things. Maybe I'll apply to one of the cafes near here or at the community college.

As I get up to leave, someone barges in, stopping me in my tracks.

It was the man from earlier.

I sit back down with quickness, making myself as small as

possible to avoid his gaze. He pays me no mind, focusing on Mr. Lance instead.

His voice was flat, detached. "I need a new secretary, immediately."

The intimidating Mr. Lance I saw at the beginning of the interview is now gone as he stumbles out of his desk to address the man.

"What happened to-"

"Do I pay you to gossip?" He interrupts. "Get me a secretary."

By now, the two have forgotten that I was in the room.

I watch silently.

He has now changed out of the suit I dirtied earlier; he didn't tower over Mr. Lance, but he was still taller. His skin was a shade darker than mine, he was sporting a full beard, and he had a low taper fade... to put it simply, he was *Fly and Fine.*

"But sir, i-it will take time, I need to...."

His head suddenly snapped towards my direction, his eyes narrowing. "She will do."

"But sir..."

"She will do."

With that, he walks out. I turn my gaze away from the door and look at Mr. Lance, "Um... what just happened?"

"Congratulations, Ms. Johnson, you are now hired to be Mr. Wyatt's new secretary."

"B-but,"

"It's five times the salary of that *custodial* job you applied for."

That's enough to get my own place by the end of the year.

I ignore the way he sneers at the word custodial, and extend my hand towards him, "When do I start?"

He ignores my hand, giving me a once-over, eyes stopping at the stain on my blouse. Sighing, he opens one of the drawers on his desk, pulls two cards out of it, and hands them to me.

"First, go to the shop on Clark Street, show them this card, and they will get you suited with something more presentable. I'll call and tell them that you're on your way."

"Thank you."

"Once dressed, meet me on the top floor. This key card will let you in the main elevator; you have 30 minutes."

"B-but,"

The shop is 20 minutes away.

"*Thirty* Minutes."

I don't complain; instead, I rush out of the office and do what I'm told. I will not let this opportunity pass. Not when I have the opportunity to finally leave that house.

Once I step outside, I let myself breathe a sigh of relief before scrambling for my phone. I dial JJ, and he picks up on the first ring.

"Wassup, baby?"

"I need help, I have less than thirty minutes to get a new outfit for my new job, and I can't take the bus because it'll take too long."

He takes a deep breath, "No can do, baby, I'm held up right now."

"Doing what?"

It's silent behind the line.

A little too silent for my taste.

"I gotta go, we still on for tonight?"

"J-"

He hangs up before I can protest.

Great. Just Great.

I look around, debating whether to take a taxi or a bus. Before I start pulling my hair out in frustration, I spot a store not too far from the office building. Without a second thought, I rush over there.

The shop was small and virtually empty, but it had exactly what I needed.

I grabbed a white blouse, identical to what I was wearing, not bothering with anything else since my skirt and tights remained intact.

I thought about getting some jewelry, but decided against it. Not having the funds.

The register was empty. I tap on the bell and call out.

"Hellooooo,"

My patience is running thin.

Please don't tell me there's no one in this store.

At the five-minute mark, I debate leaving and finding another store. Go to the original store Mr. Lance sent me or something, but I know it would be too late.

"Sorry about that, dear, my legs don't work like they used to." An older woman says with a shaky voice, breaking me out of my thoughts.

I look at the woman as she slowly makes her way to the register. She was a brown-skinned woman, her hair shaved, with prominent wrinkles across her face and hands. Seeing her wobble her way to the counter on her walker makes me feel guilty for not being more patient.

"Will that be all, dear?" She asks, scanning the blouse. I nod, my eyes on the pearls on her counter, and a picture catches my attention.

It was a wedding picture: the lady was in the center, with a young woman in a wedding dress and, I assume, her husband standing behind her, all smiling at the camera.

"That's my daughter and her husband, they got married right out of high school, it's been 3 years now."

"She's beautiful,"

Her daughter had a simple wedding dress; the cream-colored

dress looked absolutely beautiful on her dark skin, her hair straightened and down her back. Her husband was also handsome, a white man with blond hair, and he had a cheeky smile as he looked at his wife.

"And kind too, she's currently going to school to be a nurse," The older woman smiles, looking at the photo fondly. "Told her to become a doctor, but she didn't want to."

"That's cool, not a lot of us are in the health field."

"What about you, my dear?"

"Oh, I-," Her question catches me off guard. "I'm just a secretary."

She gives me a tight-lipped smile, "That'll be $33.56, dear."

Guess I'm not eating today.

I hand her my last $50 and wait patiently for the change. "Can I change in your dressing room?"

"Of course, just head to the back."

"Thank you."

Three

DESIREE

2027

"You know, it's been a while since I've been on this side of the city," Megan, Azrail's mom, comments, taking a sip of her coffee.

She and I decided to go on a shopping trip to get our kids something for their upcoming graduation.

"I used to be here all the time. This is where James' old office used to be," I comment, looking at the big building that now serves as a hotel. "There was a tiny shop right next to this coffee shop, I got lots of my clothes there, the old lady was such a lifesaver."

Megan freezes at my comment, looking at the shop I was pointing at. Which was now replaced by a flower shop.

"Was the shop called Carlines by any chance?"

I nod. "Yes, I remember the first time I went there to get a blouse, I almost went broke because it was so expensive. I thought the owner was judgmental at first, bragging about her daughter who was a nursing student and married, but giving me a side eye when I told her I didn't go to college and that I was unwed."

I stopped talking when I saw the look in her eyes. Megan and I recently became friends when her son and my daughter started dating, so I don't know her much, but the look on her face tells me something is troubling her.

"Is everything okay?"

She blinks back her tears, "Yeah, it's just that."

Taking a deep breath, she smiles at me, "That old lady was my mom."

My jaw drops at that reveal.

"Small world, right?" She comments with a smile. "She was strict and had high expectations. I didn't think she was ever that proud of me, especially since I married so young."

"Oh, she could not stop talking about you," I gush. "You know, once, she sat me down and showed me your wedding album, and high school graduation pictures. I can't believe I didn't recognize you?"

I take a closer look at her. Her long black hair, now silver locks, a few wrinkles and freckles on her face, but the same deep skin color, smile, and twinkling eyes.

Wow.

She laughs, "It's been nearly three decades. What I can't believe is that we never met. I would visit her in the store all the time."

"When I first went, she mentioned you were away in school, and then a year later the shop closed," I sigh. "I never knew what happened."

"Her health was deteriorating, so Christopher and I forced her to live with us until her last day and closed the store. She barely got any customers anyway; many people preferred the fancy stores at the mall."

"Christopher is your late husband, correct?" My mind goes back to the pictures her mom would show me, he always looked smitten by his wife.

"Yes," She smiles fondly. "He passed the day I adopted Azrail, I locked my hair in his honor."

She touches one of her locs and smiles, "He always loved learning about my hair and doing it. I decided to stop time by keeping a permanent style since his death."

"That's beautiful," I tear up. "From the pictures I saw, you loved each other deeply. I'm sorry for your loss."

"Yeah, he was a simp," She laughs at her joke. "Thank you. Sometimes my heart breaks because he never saw Azrail grow and fall in love, but I know he is watching over us and protecting us."

"I'm sure he is."

Four

DESIREE

2000

I make it back to the office with ten minutes to spare. Ignoring the judgmental looks I received from others, I went to the top floor as Mr. Lance instructed.

He was leaning down on a desk, casually flirting with the front desk personnel. I watched them for a bit. Mr. Lance wasn't ugly per se. He was an attractive, dark-skinned man, but he was short and had a balding head that just couldn't do it for me.

The young lady he was flirting with looked uncomfortable. She was a skinny young thing. Her hair styled in a pixie cut, and her skin lighter than mine, with a beauty mark next to her plump lips.

Probably feeling my stare, she makes eye contact with me and gives a genuine smile, "Hello, may I help you?"

Her words caught Mr. Lance's attention. He turned my way, his smile formed into shock before he neutralized it, "Ms. Johnson, you made it?"

So he was counting on me to fail.

"I found a shop that was closer," I smile brightly, handing him the card. "I used my own money, by the way."

Mr. Lance looks me up and down, his eyes focusing on my chest before he nods, and gathers his folders, his professional smile back on his face, "Let's get started then."

He starts walking away, and I follow him as he talks, "Mr. Wyatt is very particular about what he wants. As his secretary, your job is to correspond with his emails, transfer documents into Excel, and make his stressful life less hard."

Excel?

Mr. Lance suddenly stops mid-walk, facing me, raising a brow, "How fast can you type?"

"Um..." *I don't know.* "Pretty fast."

He sighs, rubbing his temple and muttering to himself as if he were getting a headache just talking to me. Without a word, he goes back to walking until we stop in front of a small desk.

"These papers need to be transferred electronically," He points to a huge pile. "Some on Word, some on Excel, do that asap before Mr. Wyatt's meeting at 1."

I look at the files and the clock on the desk, my eyes widening, "It's noon."

Mr. Lance looks at me like I'm dumb. "Yes, if that's all the questions you have, Ms.Johnson, I will be going now. I have work to do."

"Bu-"

He was walking away before I could finish my sentence.

I don't know how to use Excel.

It's my first day at a good-paying job, and I'm about to get fired before the day is over. I was able to transfer the files needed to

Word. In high school, we had typing classes, and although I hated it at first, I'm so glad we had that class.

I wish they had a class on Excel, but that was college-level, so I have zero experience. The documents were confusing, I had no idea where to start, and I was running out of time.

"Ms. Johnson," A deep voice on the intercom on the desk, startling me. I look at it for a minute before pressing the red button to answer.

"Y-yes,"

"Come to my office."

Mr. Wyatt's voice was monotone, no emotions at all, so I don't know what to expect. I rush to his office.

Unlike his voice, Mr. Wyatt's office actually had character, which was surprising. His desk was made with gorgeous brown oak. Behind his chair is a big, beautiful bookcase decorated with awards, some books, but they're too far for me to read the titles, and plants. Lots and lots of plants. *Well-cared-for plants.*

"Y-you called, sir?"

I mentally kick myself for the stuttering. *Way to look like a fool to your boss on your first day, Desiree.*

"What is this?"

I walk closer to him, looking at what he was pointing to on his screen, the document I transcribed and sent to him was on the screen. Not knowing what to say, I stay quiet.

He sighs at that. Apparently, that was the wrong move.

"Ms. Johnson, do you have experience with typing?"

"I do," I quickly defend myself. "I took classes in high school."

"And college..."

I look down, ashamed, feeling an embarrassing heat rise to my cheeks, "I didn't go."

He just looks at me, his face void of any emotions, like always. I couldn't tell if he was judging me.

Probably was.

"Did you finish the Excel sheets?" He changes the subject.

"Um..."

"Right, they don't teach Excel in high school," He states more to himself than to me. "Have a seat, Ms. Johnson."

I sit on the chair in front of him, tugging at my skirt in nervousness. He watches me in silence before speaking again, "I understand that you were just thrown into this role, and that is my mistake."

Oh God. I'm going to be fired.

"There are ways things are done here, Ms. Johnson," He continues. "Communication is important to the betterment of this company. If you don't know how to do something, you ask your colleague or me, you don't send half-ass bullshit that can't be fixed last minute."

"I'm sorry," My voice surprisingly strong for someone who wants to crawl into a hole and die.

"Do you understand that what you did causes more unnecessary work on my part?"

I nod quietly.

He sighs, standing up from his desk and walking towards his door without saying a word. I blink back my tears, accepting that this is his way of firing me.

I will not embarrass myself any further. Maybe that custodian job was still available.

He clears his throat, and I turn to see Mr. Wyatt looking my way, "Get up, we'll be late."

Five

JAMES

2005

"I can't do this anymore." She says, breaking the silence between us.

I stop chewing, looking at her, not surprised by her words, but disappointed she chose to say them now.

Ruining my meal.

"Can't do what exactly?" I ask, calmly, familiar with the routine.

"Be with you...be like this," She exclaims, gesturing between us.

Couples who were sitting near us tried not to make their eavesdropping obvious.

"And what exactly is this?"

"Our relationship, if I can even call it that, I want love James, not this thing that we have."

"I warned you from the beginning, Elizabeth."

But you didn't care because you enjoyed using my money.

"Yes b-,"

I cut her off: "I'm not capable of giving the love you crave."

"I know, and I thought I could handle it, but I can't," She cries, bringing more attention to us. "It's not enough."

The weekly allowances, shopping sprees, rent-free penthouse, maids, butlers, personal drivers, and assistants aren't enough?

"I understand, let's finish eating," I say, going back to my steak. Two seconds later, it was interrupted by more sniffles.

The urge to roll my eyes is strong, but I resist.

"What now?"

By now, she was twisting the diamond ring on her finger, "You're not even going to fight back?"

"You're a grown woman, perfectly capable of making your own decision. It's not my role to tell you what to do."

"We've known each other for three years, and you don't even care?"

And only dated for one, hence this dinner. *Our anniversary dinner.*

I stay silent, not liking the attraction she brings to us.

"We're engaged for fucks sake," Her voice going up a few octaves.

One thing I first liked about Elizabeth was how soft-spoken she was, even when she would yell or scream; her voice was still soft, barely audible. At first, I thought she was faking it, but later learned she's been like this all her life.

Now, I'm starting to hate it. Her soft spoken voice makes her appear weak, and me the big bully to our spectators. Like, I'm the one breaking up with her.

It doesn't help that I tower over her, and the fact that she's a petite girl and I'm the 'stereotypical' mean-looking man.

"We were." I corrected. "You can keep the ring."

She scoffs, packing up her things and getting up.

"You're going to end up alone if you don't change your behavior, James Wyatt."

I roll my eyes and continue eating as she leaves, ignoring the stares. I know what they're thinking.

This guy let the attractive girl walk away crying.

Something must be wrong with him.

Six

DESIREE

2005

The sounds of my heels echo through the hall as I make my way to my office, grabbing everyone's attention as I walk past. I respond to their greetings with a nod and a small smile.

In my office, I'm greeted by two bouquets of flowers, Daisies and red roses. Rolling my eyes, I throw both in the trash, not caring to check the card.

Grabbing the files on my desk, I get ready to start my day. Before I make it two steps out of the office, I'm immediately stopped by one of Mr. Wyatt's assistants.

He stutters a bit before clearing his throat to try again. I plaster a fake smile.

To think, five years ago, they wouldn't give me the light of day. Now they spill over themselves to get in my good graces.

Annoying.

"Ms. Johnson,"

"What's the damage?" I asked before he could finish. The tension in the office is clear enough.

"I don't know, he's just mad."

"He's always mad."

"Madder than usual"

With a sigh, I walk faster to his office. Blake, the worker who was with me, stops following and screams out, "By the way, Happy Anniversary, Ms.Johnson."

I don't respond. Instead, I take another deep breath, put on a fake smile, and open the office door.

"Good Morning, Mr. Wyatt," I start, getting ready to go over his schedule for the day.

"Ah..." A voice stops me on my track, "Good morning, Ms. Johnson,"

I look up, a genuine smile coating my lips when my eyes fall on Marcus.

"Oh, Mr. Hale, didn't see you there, good morning."

"How's my favorite secretary doing? This old grump isn't being too harsh, huh?"

"Nothing I can't handle." I wink, laughing a bit.

At that, Mr. Wyatt finally speaks, "This old grump is right here?"

"Don't mind him, Desiree. He's just heartbroken that his girlfriend broke up with him."

I pause, glancing at him, raising a brow. He says nothing.

Elizabeth wasn't my favorite, a little too annoying for my taste, but she was such a sweet girl. Always bringing me sweets, compared to his other girlfriends, who saw me as the help or were threatened by me, she saw me as an acquaintance and was nice.

"Not heartbroken, just annoyed at my time being wasted." Mr. Wyatt huffs, not even looking up at us.

"Sorry to hear that, you must've really loved her, sir."

He stops typing at my words, finally looking in my direction, raising a brow, "Love?"

"I mean, to propose so fast must mean you love her, right?" He proposed to her 6 months into the relationship.

Marcus laughs, "Now Desiree, you know this man knows nothing about 'love', he only proposed because it was his 'duty'."

"Oh." *I should've known.*

Mr. Wyatt sends a glare to Marcus, "Weren't you just leaving?"

"Right, right. Happy Anniversary, Desiree."

I nod, "Thank you."

After he walks out, I return to my original duty, listing off Mr. Wyatt's schedule and tasks, as he listened quietly.

"Daisy?"

My heart tightens at that. I've been working for him for five years, *five years,* and he still doesn't remember my name.

"Yes, sir?"

"What did you mean by oh?"

I blink.

"I'm not sure I understand your question."

"Earlier," His voice monotoned as always. "When talking to Marcus, you said, ' Oh, ' when he told you why I proposed. What did you mean?"

"Um..."

"You can be honest, Daisy."

"I was just surprised, that's all," I answer cautiously. "I didn't think you would be the type to marry because of duty, not love."

He stays silent for a beat before going back to his computer, "Check your email once you're in the office, there are a couple of changes I need you to make for our meeting this evening."

"Yes, sir," I nod, walking out.

Seven

JAMES

2005

"Did you see how much work he's given her today?"

"Yeah, she will be working overtime for sure."

"On her anniversary? It's been five years, you would think she would get better treatment by now." "Come on, guys, if she had a problem with it, I'm sure she would've said something."

"Yeah, right, who in their right mind would speak up to that brute? Have you seen his face?"

Their laughter was cut off short when I walked past, fear radiating off of them. They are waiting for me to cause a scene, but I say nothing instead. I make my way to her office.

I gave two knocks before opening the door. Daisy was sitting behind her desk, engrossed in what was on her screen.

"Daisy, I need you to convert these files for me before you leave."

She nods, one of her messy curls falling on her forehead. Her hair was messier than when she first came in; instead of the original bun she had, she sported a messier look with her hair out of its hold and cascading down in a wild manner.

I noticed she had a habit of never leaving her hair up in its original style; it's always back to its afro style by lunch, no matter how complicated the style was.

"Mr. Moreau called earlier. He wants to know if you will be attending ***The Whitemore Foundation Gala*** next Saturday?"

I always skip that Gala, but this year is different.

I give her a simple nod, my eyes falling to the trash can by her desk, where two crushed bouquets lie. I feel myself lingering in her office more than necessary, but I couldn't help myself.

Her voice brings my attention back to her, "Can I help you with anything else, Mr. James?"

"No need to come to the office tomorrow." I absentmindedly state, walking out of her office before she could reply.

The Next Day

"You seriously asked for marriage six months in? Why?"

I roll my eyes at Adrian's exclamation. He has been out of the country these past few months, and Marcus was catching him up on my life.

In my office.

During office hours.

I shrug, "It's time to settle down."

He looks skeptical of my answer, "Mhm, is that all?"

Both of them were judging me, I could tell by the way Marcus was silent, and Adrian's brow furrowed.

"Yes," I lie, because if they knew the truth, they wouldn't like it.

Adrian sighs out loud, "Still, James, that's not how you go about it."

"What do you mean?"

Marcus lets out a bigger sigh, running his fingers on his face, "I can't. Where's Ms. Johnson? Maybe she can explain it to him."

Adrian answers before I could, "You know she's not here, she's always off on the day after her anniversary."

He's a very perceptive. I hate that at times.

"Why do you need Daisy?" My question surprises me.

Both Marcus and Adrian look at each other and sigh out loud. They look at me like I'm a child who doesn't understand social cues.

I hate that at times.

Well, at least I think I do.

Noticing my slight irritation, although I'm confident it's not explicitly showing on my face, Adrian explains, "She is one of the few people who can explain things in a way you understand."

Is that so?

"That's because he basically groomed her to understand him."

I glare at Marcus. I don't like that word.

Groomed.

But in a way, he is right. When she first started working with me, everyone called her a lost cause.

She could barely type 100 words per minute, overexplained everything, and was insecure about anything she did. Now, she is precise, fast, and confident.

If I could, I would say I feel proud. Very proud.

"Okay...." Adrian says mitigating us before a fight could start. "Why don't we change the subject? James, how's business?"

The air in the office changed at his words. Marcus leans closer, his playful demeanor gone.

"They're asking for more security for the next shipping," I answer, "The Japanese ambushed them last time, and a lot of supplies were lost."

"I didn't know the Japanese were involved. Why the fuck didn't they tell us?" Marcus scowled, frustrated by the new fact.

I share the same frustration.

Those fuckers didn't tell us the truth, and because of that, the deal went bad, and we look unreliable to our other customers. I was ready to cut ties with them, but they upped their price. It would be dumb to lose on such a business deal.

"The Japanese asked to work with us," Adrian states, "I told them I would bring it up to you all first."

Shit.

"When did that happen?"

"I stayed there for two weeks during my travels, for another business venture."

Shit. Shit.

"Good thing you're retiring, James, so you don't have to deal with this bullshit anymo-"

"What's with that look?" Adrian interrupted Marcus

Always perceptive. "I'm not retiring anymore,"

"Huh? Why not?"

"Since I'm not getting married anytime soon, I figured what's the point?" I shrug.

They're both quiet for a beat. Looking at each other as if they're communicating telepathically.

"I don't like when you guys do that."

"Do what?"

"Have private conversations about me to my face," I growl. "If you have something to say, just fucking say it."

Before they could respond, Lance barged into the office, "Mr. Wyatt, the Whitlocks are here to meet with you."

Adrian groans, "That's my cue to leave, before those fuckers see me."

Marcus quipped, "Why?" with a raised brow.

"They're desperate to adopt."

"What's that got to do with you?"

"They want to use my connections for it," He groans more dramatically. "And that woman doesn't take no for an answer."

"I'm surprised they're looking to adopt, I don't see them loving a child that isn't biological theirs."

"Word on the street, the Mrs. doesn't want to ruin her perfect figure, and she's too jealous for surrogacy."

Speaking of the devil. Mrs. and Mr. Whitlock barged into my office, almost hitting Lance. Mrs. Whitlock's eyes fall on Adrian immediately, a sultry smile on her lips, whilst her husband isn't looking.

Her lips stained red, "Mr. Cole, what a pleasure."

I spoke before he could respond, sending a glare at the bald man in front of my desk, "Mr. Whitlock, when did I give you the impression that you could barge into my office?"

He tries to keep his intimidating posture to save face, but one look at his red face, and I know it's a lie. At my words, Adrian visibly relaxes while Vanessa scurries next to her husband like a dog.

"Don't be like that, James," She drags out my name like it was a foreign language. "Our family has a deep history. We're basically cousins."

"With all due respect, *Vanessa*," She huffs at my mocking of her voice. "My family doesn't represent me."

"Yet, you still use their last name." Mr. Whitlock mumbles under his breath. I chose to ignore his passing comment, but Marcus decided otherwise.

"What was that, Harold?" He sneers, getting up from his seat and walking towards him, his height and frame towering over the coward.

Harold stutters out a quick nothing, lowering his eyes. His wife clears her throat, putting on a huge plastic smile on her face before sitting on the chair in front of my desk and dragging her husband down with her.

"Look, we're here to make sure you hold your end of the bargain. We haven't heard anything from you, and my people are impatient."

By his people, he means his debtor. Harold tends to gamble and make poor decisions with his businesses. All he has to himself is the privilege of his name and skin color.

I raise a brow, getting tired of their presence, "Have I ever backed out of a deal?"

"N-no, I-"

"Then why are you really here, Harold?"

"It's about the Gala, we all know Moreau is a family man, and it's hard to get on his good side without that."

I stay quiet, waiting for him to get to his useless point. After a few seconds of uncomfortable silence, he clears his throat and continues, "The news about your unfortunate outcome with Elizabeth was brought to my attention by a mutual colleague."

"Get on with it, Harold," Marcus interrupts, earning a slight laugh from Adrian. Vanessa glares at them for a quick second, but quickly adds her fake smile when she sees my blank face.

"What my husband wants to suggest is a business deal," She speaks for them both. "A business relationship with my niece so you could get on Moreau's good graces."

"How does it benefit you?"

"Her father, my brother, recently passed, and in his will, she isn't allowed company stocks without being married."

I already knew this. I'm surprised she told the truth.

"And you are one of the few we could trust not to take over the company completely, despite your reputation, I am inclined to believe that you would respect her and allow her to have control of her shares."

"*My reputation.*"

Vanessa turns red in embarrassment at my words.

"What my *wife* means to say," Harold glares at her and speaks through gritted teeth. "Is that, we trust you and think this arrangement would be great for all parties involved."

And you want my bank account to help your family.

"Not interested."

They flinch at my coldness, Marcus laughs.

"What he means is," Adrian tries to help. "It's too soon for a marriage; it won't look right for your niece."

"Why don't you attend the Gala with her, get to know her?"

They were getting desperate, I saw it in their eyes. "She's a nice girl," Vanessa continues.

Before responding, I see Adrian sending me a warning look. "I...," I try to think of an excuse. "I already have a date."

"You do?" Marcus and the Whitlocks echo while Adrian just shakes his head in defeat.

"I do," I confirm, standing up. "I have a meeting, let's keep these impromptu meetings to a minimum."

Before anyone could say anything, I left my office, my feet walking to a place where no one would disturb me.

Daisy's Office.

Eight

DESIREE

2005

It's been five years since I started working for James, and I still don't know what to do on the rare occasions I get a day off.

I thought about contacting my siblings, but they have their family to take care of and live far away, and the one who does live close...Let's just say I would rather die than hang out with her.

Deciding not to wallow around, I make a day of it doing my favorite thing.

Treating myself.

Putting on a nice dress and light makeup, I made my way out. Before leaving, I look around my apartment, it's smaller than the room I had in my parents' house, but it's mine, and that's all I care about. All mine. Not theirs.

I smile at that thought. I'm proud of myself. The changes I made in my life got me a bachelor's degree, a well-paying job, and my own place, all on my own. Without my family's money.

In your face, Mom.

I first make my way to a book shop, my favorite author just

came out with book three of her series, and with work I haven't had time to buy it. The shop is small and very cozy.

The owners were this mother-daughter duo. The daughter, a shy pre-teen, would always give me the best recommendations when I came, and in return, I would do her hair.

"Daisy, sweetheart," Ms. Carter calls, wobbling over to me on her cane. "You're here early."

"I don't have work today, figure I'd come by and see what you have." Bending down, I give her a kiss on the cheek and head straight to the new releases section.

Once I got my books and bade goodbye, I made my way to a cafe down the street. I sit by the window with a latte and begin reading, allowing myself to exist without rushing. After that, I wander into a beauty supply store and buy a face mask I definitely don't need, then stop at a nail salon for a manicure.

By the time I'm walking back to my car, my phone buzzes.

AUNT LORRAINE

Hey baby! Just checking in. Your cousin's wedding is in three weeks, can't wait to see you! Are you dating anyone yet?

I groan.

Another text comes in before I can respond.

You're not getting any younger, you know. It'd be nice to see you bring someone this time.

I stare at the screen, irritation bubbling up.

Here we go.

I don't even reply.

Instead, I do something impulsive.

I downloaded a dating app.

Actually, two. Everyone's talking about them anyway.

I set up a profile, upload a decent picture, and tell myself this isn't serious.

I just need a wedding date.
That's it.

The Next Day

"Ms. Johnson."

His voice comes from the intercom on my desk.

"Coming."

Standing up, I smooth my skirt automatically and walk to his office, already preparing myself for whatever he is going to ask me today.

"Yes, sir?"

"Did you RSVP for the Gala already?" He asks, not looking up from his papers.

"Yes," I nod. "I also sent your suit to the dry cleaners. It will be dropped off at your penthouse tomorrow."

"I need you to change the RSVP."

"Are you not planning on going anymore?"

That wouldn't be shocking; he seldom attends these things.

"No, I'm bringing a plus one."

I nod, asking no further questions. We stay silent for a bit before he gets up and stands in front of his desk, leaning back a bit, arms crossed.

"My friends said something yesterday," he begins. "Something I don't fully understand."

That's... new.

"They implied I approach relationships incorrectly."

I stare.

"Can I be honest, sir?" I ask carefully, "With no retaliation?"

He studies me for a moment, then nods.

"I believe your emotional blindness is the cause," I say slowly, cautiously. "You see things through logic, but that's not what a woman wants to hear. A woman wants romance. She wants to be wooed. Being told, *'I want to marry because it's time to settle down'* isn't romantic."

He says nothing.

I continue, emboldened by his silence. "Love isn't efficient. It's emotional. Messy. Illogical."

Another pause.

"Thank you for your honesty," he finally says.

"And," I add, trying to soften the blow, "I don't think you need to pressure yourself so much, Mr. Wyatt. You're still young. Don't rush into things. Just... have fun."

He looks at me sharply. "Is that what you do, Ms. Johnson?"

I pause, then shrug. "Not really. I only date when I want my family to get off my back. Like right now."

His brow furrows.

"I'm going on a date after work with someone I met last night on a dating app," I admit for some reason. "Just to see if I can bring him to my cousin's wedding."

He stays silent for a beat. A wave of confusion in his features.

"A dating app?"

"Yeah," I say lightly. "eHarmony. Match.com. It's all the rage now."

He clears his throat, removing his glasses to clean them. "Daisy, you need to learn how to be more assertive with your family. Take charge."

I smile faintly. "Easier said than done, Mr. Wyatt."

He doesn't agree but also doesn't disagree. We just stare at each other, nothing awkward, just an air of understanding between us.

And for the first time since working for him, I feel a slight change between us.

Nine

JAMES

2005

"I need your help."

Adrian looks up from his glass, already annoyed. "With what?"

"With getting a wife."

Marcus chokes on his whiskey.

Adrian blinks.

Once.

Twice.

"Man, what the hell is going on with you?"

"It's time for me to settle down."

"No," Adrian says immediately. "Nope. I can't help you."

"Why not?"

"Why me?" he shoots back.

Daisy's words from yesterday echo in my head, love isn't efficient, it's emotional.

"Daisy mentioned that to marry, I have to be romantic, not logical," I say evenly. "And logically, you're the most romantic person I know."

Marcus scoffs. "Wow."

"And Marcus," I continue, "is a whore. He doesn't know anything about romance."

"Ouch," Marcus says, offended. "You're right, but ouch."

I take a sip of my rum, letting the burn ground me.

Before either of them can respond, my office door opens.

"Mr. Wyatt," Daisy says, already walking in, tablet in hand. "These contracts need your signature, and the shipment schedules were updated. Also, Mr. Moreau's assistant called again."

She moves easily through the space, placing papers where I need them, adjusting my calendar without me asking. I sign where she points. Adrian and Marcus watch us as we work in silence, quickly and seamlessly.

"Anything else?" she asks.

"No."

She nods once and leaves, heels clicking softly as the door shuts behind her.

Marcus lets out a low whistle. "Well, damn."

"I have an idea," He says.

"I'm afraid to ask," Adrian mutters.

"Why don't you ask Desiree for help?"

"That's a terrible idea," I say instantly.

"That's a great idea," Adrian counters.

"Why?" I ask with an air of irritation in my voice.

Adrian leans forward. "She's a hopeless romantic. She knows you. She tolerates you. And you two work disturbingly well together."

"And she's hot," Marcus adds.

"Marcus," I warn.

"I'm just saying," he shrugs. "Listen to me, James. Daisy's the perfect person to help you. She wouldn't mind."

"How do you know she's a hopeless romantic?"

Marcus smirks. "Her office."

My jaw tightens. "You've been in her office?"

"It's see-through," he says quickly. "Relax. I walked past one day and saw her reading one of those romance novels every woman's obsessed with now. Something about a vampire or some shit."

Adrian nods. "Marcus has a point. And who knows, maybe with her help, you'll find your wife without even realizing it."

They exchange a look.

I don't understand it. I don't like it.

"I'll think about it," I say, ending the conversation.

Later, alone in my office, my eyes drift to the empty doorway.

And for the first time, the idea doesn't feel completely illogical.

Daisy

The date was awful.

Not awkward-but-okay awful. Not maybe-he-was-nervous awful.

Just awful.

He talked about himself the entire time, complained about his ex, made a joke about my hair that I don't think he meant to be insulting but absolutely was, and then asked if I planned on quitting my job once I got married.

I smiled through it. Finished my drink. Lied about an early morning.

And the moment I got home, I kicked off my heels, discarded my bra, turned on my phone, and deleted all the dating profiles without hesitation.

So much for modern romance.

I spent the rest of the night staring at my ceiling, mentally drafting excuses for my cousin's wedding.

Work emergency.

Sudden illness.

Out of the country.

None of them felt convincing enough to survive my aunt's interrogation.

I was halfway through my emails when the intercom buzzed. "Ms. Johnson."

I exhale. "Coming."

I walk to his office, confused about why he needed me again, under the impression that everything was dealt with when I came by earlier.

Once entering his office, he looks up briefly and gestures for me to sit in the chair in front of him.

I do.

We sit in silence for a bit before he speaks. "How was your date?"

I blinked.

"...Bad," I admit, then groan before I can stop myself. "Horrible. A complete waste of time. I don't know why I even bothered."

He looks at me more attentively.

"He talked over me, judged everything, and somehow made my job his problem," I continue, irritation spilling out. "I deleted my profile. I'd rather go to the wedding alone than suffer through that again."

Silence.

"I have a proposition, Daisy."

His words make my stomach tighten.

"You need help," he continues. "And I need help."

I frown. "You do? I do?"

"Yes," he says simply. "You need a date for your cousin's wedding. I need someone to help me get a wife."

I laugh once, sharply. "I'm sorry....what?"

"It's a win-win," he says calmly, as if proposing a business merger. "You accompany me to the gala. In return, you advise me. Coach me."

"Coach you... How to date?"

"How to love," he corrects.

I shake my head. "B-but—"

He stands, walking around his desk and turning my chair to face him.

Then he takes my hand.

The contact is firm, deliberate. He looks down at me, his expression still unreadable with a hint of uncertainty.

"Teach me, Daisy," he says quietly. "Teach me how to love. *Please.*"

My heart stutters.

Everything in me is screaming to pull away, to set a clear boundary.

And yet... the man standing in front of me doesn't look powerful or untouchable. Instead, he looks lost, desperate, and confused.

I swallow.

"I'll think about it," I say, gently pulling my hand back.

But as I walk out of his office, one thought repeats itself, loud and insistent:

You already know the answer.

JAMES

2027

Daisy and I still go on dates.

After all these years, after vows, a mortgage, and a daughter who somehow went from scraped knees to college acceptance letters (she still scrapes her knee).

Every Friday. No exceptions unless the world is ending.

And if the world were ending, I would be by her side.

Tonight, it's a small Italian place tucked between a bookstore and a florist. Nothing flashy.

Candlelit, quiet.

She's wearing yellow.

I watch her as she talks more than I do. *It's always like this.*

Her hands move when she laughs, expressive, animated, still just as incapable of staying still as they were twenty years ago when she sat across from my desk.

Our food arrives, and somewhere between the wine and dessert, we start reminiscing.

"Can you believe she's leaving in two months?" Daisy says,

shaking her head with a soft laugh. "I swear, yesterday she was five, asking us to check under her bed for monsters."

"She asked me that at twelve," I remind her.

"She was testing you," she smiles. "You passed.

"I already miss her," My wife admits, swirling the wine in her glass. "The house is going to feel so quiet."

I reach across the table and lace my fingers through hers. Her ring catches the candlelight.

"We can always move closer to her," I say simply.

She looks at me, flashing me her beautiful smile, like she always does when I do something to make her happy.

"We should," she agrees.

Later at home, the night settles around us the way it always does—quiet, comfortable, ours.

The front door barely closes before Daisy is laughing again, that same bright sound that has undone me for twenty years. She slips off her shoes near the entryway, leaning back against the wall for balance. The hem of her yellow dress rides just slightly up her thigh.

"You're doing it again," she says, folding her arms loosely.

"Doing what?"

"That thing where you look like you're evaluating a security risk."

"I am."

Her eyebrow lifts. "And what exactly is the threat?"

"You," I answer simply.

She laughs under her breath, shaking her head as she walks closer. Slow steps. Deliberate.

"That's a new one," she says. "Usually I'm the one accusing you of being dangerous."

"You are."

"And yet you married me."

"I assessed the risk and accepted it."

She stops right in front of me now, close enough that the scent of her perfume, something soft and warm, fills the space between us.

"Accepted it?" she repeats, amused. "That's very romantic, James."

"It was a calculated decision."

"Oh?" Her fingers slide up the front of my jacket, straightening my collar like she's done a thousand times. "And what were the variables?"

"You," I say.

She tilts her head. "That's not very specific."

"It didn't need to be."

Her smile widens slightly, the way it always does when she knows she's winning.

"You know," she murmurs, "most husbands take their wives to dinner and then say something sweet afterward."

"I did say something sweet."

"You called me a security threat."

"You are distracting," I correct calmly.

Her hand pauses on my chest.

"Distracting," she repeats.

"Yes."

Her eyes narrow playfully.

"James Wyatt... are you flirting with me?"

"I have been married to you for twenty years," I say. "It would be inefficient to stop now."

She laughs again, soft this time, and steps even closer, until there's barely any space left between us.

"You've gotten bold in your old age."

"I was always bold."

"Please," she scoffs lightly. "You used to analyze our conversations like they were business negotiations."

"They were important negotiations."

Her fingers slide down to my tie, slowly tugging it loose.

"And now?"

"Now I already won."

That earns me a look.

The kind that's half challenge, half heat.

"You're very confident tonight."

"I'm observant," I reply.

Her lips curve, "And what exactly have you observed?"

"That you wore yellow tonight."

She glances down at the dress, then back up at me.

"Yes..."

"I love that color on you."

She smiles.

"Is that so?"

"Yes."

"James."

"Yes?"

"You're staring again."

"I warned you."

She exhales a quiet laugh, her forehead briefly touching my chest before she looks back up at me.

"You're impossible."

"And yet," I murmur, sliding a hand around her waist, "you're still here."

Her hands settle against my shoulders.

"Maybe I just like impossible things."

"Convenient."

Her eyes flick down to my mouth for half a second.

Then back up.

"Are you going to kiss me," she asks softly, "or keep analyzing the situation?"

"I'm gathering data."

"You've had twenty years of data."

"Not tonight's."

My thumb brushes the bare skin at her back where the dress dips low. Her breath catches—barely noticeable unless you know her the way I do.

And I do.

Twenty years have taught me every small reaction her body gives away.

Her hands slide up my chest slowly, deliberately. Not hurried. Never hurried. We've long since learned there is no reason to rush anything between us.

"James," she says softly.

It's half a warning. Half invitation.

My mouth brushes her temple first. Then her cheek.

By the time I reach her lips, she's already leaning into me.

The kiss is slow at first. Familiar. Warm.

Then it deepens.

Her fingers curl into the front of my shirt as if she's forgotten we've done this a thousand times before. As if it still surprises her how easily we fall back into this rhythm.

By the time we make it upstairs, the years between our first kiss and tonight feel nonexistent. We still know exactly how to undo each other without saying a word.

Afterward, Daisy falls asleep curled into my side, one leg thrown over mine, her breathing slow and even.

She's always fallen asleep faster than I do.

I trace idle patterns across her back, feeling the rise and fall of each breath beneath my palm. The warmth of her body against mine.

Grounding myself in the weight of her.

The reality of her.

Madly doesn't even cover how in love I am with her.

I press a slow kiss into her hair.

I am madly, hopelessly, relentlessly in love with my wife.

My phone vibrates on the nightstand, interrupting my thoughts.

At first, I don't move. It's late. Anyone who knows me knows better than to contact me now.

Except for three people.

I carefully shift, making sure Daisy doesn't wake, and reach for the phone.

ADRIAN

I got it.

I give Daisy one last glance before dialing his number and walking out of the room.

Eleven

JAMES

2005

They stared at me as if I had just announced I was selling the company to a stranger I met on the street.

"She said yes?"

Adrian's voice echoed slightly in the penthouse, bouncing off glass walls. Marcus was seated on the arm of the couch, whiskey forgotten in his hand, mouth actually hanging open. That alone should've been enough to irritate me.

"Yes," I said, straightening the cuff of my shirt. "She said yes."

"To *that*?" Marcus asked, finally finding his voice. "You didn't even frame it as normal, James. You basically asked her to emotionally rehabilitate you."

I rolled my eyes. "I asked her to help me understand love."

"That's worse," Adrian muttered. "That's so much worse."

They'd been like this for ten minutes now. Shock. Disbelief. Thinly veiled concern, as if Daisy Johnson had just agreed to assist me in committing some unspeakable crime instead of... whatever this was.

Marcus leaned forward. "Okay, but what exactly did you say to her?"

I paused. Considered lying. But decided against it.

"I told her I needed help. That she needed help. That it was mutually beneficial."

Adrian pressed his fingers to his temple. "You didn't, at any point, consider that this might be wildly inappropriate?"

"She's an adult," I said flatly. "And she had the option to say no."

"And yet she said yes," Marcus said slowly. "That's the part that's fucking with me."

I shrugged. "I don't see the issue."

"The issue," Adrian said, standing now, pacing toward the windows, "is that you are her boss. Her *very intimidating* boss. And she just agreed to... teach you how to love."

"I didn't threaten her," I snapped.

"No," Adrian agreed. "You just cornered her emotionally after a bad date and asked her to be your romantic mentor."

Marcus winced. "When you put it like that-"

"Stop putting it like anything," I cut in. "She agreed because she wanted to. End of discussion."

They exchanged a look.

That look.

The one I hated.

Marcus sighed. "You know what? Fine. Let's say this is all aboveboard. What's the first step, oh great emotionally stunted one?"

I checked my watch.

"I'm going to her apartment."

That did it.

Adrian spun around. "You're doing *what*?"

"She said the first lesson starts tonight."

Marcus barked out a laugh. "Absolutely not. No. That's a terrible idea."

"Why?" I asked, already grabbing my coat.

"Because," Adrian said slowly, "you don't go to your secretary's apartment alone at night to learn about romance. That's how PR nightmares are born."

"I don't have PR," I replied coolly.

"At this point, you need to"

I don't respond, already heading for the elevator.

Behind me, Marcus calls out, "If you come back quoting poetry or some shit, I'm disowning you."

The elevator doors closed before I could hear the rest.

Daisy lived across town, in a neighborhood I'd only ever driven through without really seeing.

I parked and sat in the car longer than necessary.

This was ridiculous, I told myself. It was a lesson. No different than learning a new language or negotiating a deal. I was here to observe, absorb, and apply.

That was all.

Her building was modest. Brick. Clean. I rang the bell marked *J. Johnson*.

A few seconds passed.

Then the door buzzed open. I make my way to the second floor as she instructed. Seconds later, she answers the door, stepping aside to let me in.

Her apartment is cozy. Warm lighting. Books everywhere, on shelves, stacked on tables, one face down on the arm of the couch. The faint smell of vanilla and something floral lingered in the air.

She stood barefoot by her door, wearing soft pants and an oversized sweater, her hair loose and wild around her shoulders.

"This is... informal," I said before I could stop myself.

She smiled. "We're watching rom-coms, not negotiating a merger."

I frowned. "Romantic comedies?"

"Yes."

She gestured for me to sit. I chose the armchair instead of the couch to maintain distance.

"Okay," she said, clapping her hands once. "Lesson one."

I folded my arms. "I'm listening."

She grabbed a stack of DVDs from the coffee table.

"You need context," she said. "Rom-coms are exaggerated, yes, but they show emotional beats clearly. They teach timing, vulnerability, gestures."

"Gestures," I repeated skeptically.

"Yes. Effort. Intention."

She popped a disc into the player. The screen flickered to life.

"What are we watching?" I asked.

"When Harry Met Sally."

I stared at the screen. "That's from the eighties."

"And still relevant," she shot back. "Which is lesson number two: good love stories age well."

I say nothing.

We watch in silence at first. I analyzed it the way I analyzed everything: dialogue patterns, cause and effect, conflict escalation.

Halfway through, I spoke. "They're incompatible."

She paused the movie and looked at me like I'd insulted her personally.

"They're scared," she corrected. "There's a difference."

I frowned. "Fear is irrational."

"So is love."

She let that sit.

By the second movie, *Notting Hill,* she'd moved onto the couch closer to my chair. She even started throwing popcorn at me when I criticized the premise.

"You can't just walk into a bookstore every day hoping to see the same woman," I argued.

"That's the point," she said. "He hopes."

"Hoping is inefficient."

She laughed. Full, unguarded. It did something strange to my chest.

"Mr. Wyatt," she said gently, "romance isn't about efficiency. It's about showing up even when it doesn't make sense."

I watched the screen. Julia Roberts smiled. The man stuttered through a declaration of love.

"I'm just a girl," she said. "Standing in front of a boy, asking him to love her."

"That's manipulative," I muttered.

Daisy threw a pillow at my head.

By the third movie, something had shifted.

I found myself less critical. Less defensive. Watching the way characters reached for each other, failed, and tried again. I didn't fully understand it. But I could see the pattern. Risk. Reward. Vulnerability.

At some point, she asked, "What scares you about relationships?"

I answered immediately. "I don't know."

She nods. Silence settled comfortably around us.

When the last credits rolled, she stretched, yawning. "So. Homework."

I straightened. "Homework?"

"Yes. Observation exercise."

I waited.

"Next time you interact with someone you're interested in," she said, "don't lead with logic. Lead with curiosity. Ask questions without an agenda."

"That sounds inefficient," I said automatically.

She smiled. "You're learning."

I stood, suddenly aware of the time. "Thank you. For this."

She looked surprised. Then softened.

"You're welcome."

At the door, I paused. "A driver will pick you up tomorrow."

She met my gaze and gave a slight nod.

DESIREE

2005

The dress arrived the morning before the Gala.

It didn't come with a card or a note, but in a big garment bag so heavy that I had to drag it inside with both hands. I stared at it for a full minute in my entryway before I exhaled a long, tired breath.

One thing I've learned over the past five years of working for him is that Mr. Wyatt didn't do *subtle* when it came to logistics. Or money for that matter.

Inside the bag was a dress the color of late-summer honey, and silk that caught the light, cut to follow the body without clinging. Elegant. Beautiful. *Expensive.*

I touched the fabric with two fingers, then immediately pulled my hand back, as if it might bite.

"No," I said out loud to my empty apartment. "Absolutely not."

I closed the garment bag, then reopened it because I couldn't stop looking at the dress.

The dress was beautiful. But expensive. Even with the price tag not attached, I just knew it was more expensive than I could ever imagine.

I'm used to expensive things. I grew up around wealth, went to a private school, lived in a big house, but James. James wealth is different, it's generational, and from what I know.... kind of illegal.

I take my phone and call him. He answers right away. "You got the dress."

"Yes," I said tightly. "And I can't accept it."

A pause.

Even though I couldn't see him, I knew that he was contemplating what I said. Assessing my words.

"Why not?"

"Because," I said, folding my arms, "you're not supposed to buy your fake date couture gowns."

"Why?"

I blinked. "Because it defeats the point."

I hear him lean back in his chair. "Explain."

I exhaled slowly. "You can't buy love with money, Mr. Wyatt."

"I'm not buying love."

"You're trying to spoil me into compliance."

"I don't need your compliance," he said calmly. "I already have your agreement."

He got me there.

"That's not the same thing." My voice is not as strong as it was earlier.

"No," he conceded. "But it is related."

I shook my head. "This is supposed to be... normal. Equal. You're already my boss. If you start throwing money at me—"

"I have a lesson for you, Ms. Johnson," he interrupted, catching me off guard.

His voice lower than usual. "A real man," he said evenly, "will always want to spoil a beautiful woman."

I opened my mouth to speak, but quickly closed it, not knowing what to say.

"And," he added, "he will do so not as leverage, but as expression. Accept it."

I say nothing for a beat.

"So this is not you just spoiling me," I say carefully, trying to understand him. "This is you trying to manage optics."

"Correct," he said. "The Gala requires presentation. This dress fulfills that requirement."

"And if I don't wear it?"

He didn't hesitate. "Then I will return it."

That... surprised me.

No argument. No pressure. The man I dated would get offended if I didn't wear their gifts.

Well, you aren't dating.

I sighed. "Fine. I'll wear it. But this doesn't mean I owe you anything."

"I'm aware," he said. "You just owe me lessons. That's already agreed upon."

I rolled my eyes and bid my goodbyes before hanging up.

The car arrived exactly at seven.

A quiet man in a suit opens the car door without comment and waits with a blank expression.

Once we arrived and I stepped out of the car, the city air felt different, crisper, and charged. I adjusted the warp over my shoulders.

The Whitemore Foundation Gala was everything I expected it to be: glass and gold, champagne flutes catching light, laughter polished to a shine. Wealth humming beneath every interaction like a second language. It reminds me of the parties described in The Great Gatsby.

James was waiting near the entrance.

For a moment, I freeze.

The tux was tailored within an inch of its life. Black, sharp, restrained. His hair was neatly styled, his posture impeccable as always. But it was his expression that stopped me.

Focused. Alert. And, when his eyes found mine, I swear I saw something softer beneath them.

He took one step forward.

"You look-"

He stopped himself.

Then, more carefully: "You look appropriate."

I laughed despite myself. "High praise."

He offered his arm. I hesitated only a second before taking it.

I catch my reflection on the door as we walk towards it. The fabric of the dress skimmed my skin, and the color warmed my tone. We looked like a real couple.

We stepped inside together.

Immediately, heads turn. I felt it, the shift, the recalibration. People assessing, cataloging, deciding if I fit.

James leaned down slightly. "Another lesson," he murmured. "Walk like you belong."

I thought I was the only teacher between us.

"I do belong," I said quietly.

"I know," he replied. "I want you to remind them."

We moved through the crowd smoothly. His hands snake around my waist, grounding me. Some of his clients who know me as his secretary look at us in surprise, and those who don't look confused, trying to figure out who I am.

"James!" Marcus's voice cut through the din.

He approached with a grin that screamed *trouble*, champagne already in hand. Adrain followed, eyes lighting up when he saw me.

"Well," Adrain drawled, "if this isn't a surprise."

"Good evening," I said politely.

"Hi, Dais-"

"It's Desiree."

The correction was sharp. Immediate.

So he does know my name.

James didn't even look at Marcus when he said it; he was typing something on his phone. The air shifted.

Marcus blinked. Once. Then lifted his brows. "Desiree. Of course."

Adrian hid a smile behind his glass.

Before the conversation could continue, someone stopped in front of me. "Ms. Johnson pleasure to see you here."

I smile, letting him take my hand in mind. "Pleasure is all mine, Mr. Walker."

Mr. Walker is a police officer and is also in charge of all security personnel at the gala today. From what I've observed in the past five years, he also occasionally helps Mr. Wyatt train his body-guards and other stuff I'm not allowed to know about.

Company secret. But it doesn't take a genius to guess.

"James, why force your beautiful secretary to come to this Gala tonight. You should've given her the night off." He says, giving me a teasing smile before mock glaring at Mr.Wyatt.

Mr. Walker is also one of the few, besides Marcus, who speaks to my boss like that.

Before I could correct him, I felt the hand around my waist, pull me gently until my back hit his chest. I look up at him, trying to mask my shock.

"*Howard,*" He starts, voice monotoned as usual. "Daisy is my date tonight, not my *employee.*"

I watch as Officer Walker's eyebrow shoots up. "Oh."

"And in the future," Mr. Wyatt continues. "Let's leave the concern of *my* employees to *me.*"

Marcus whistled. "Well, damn."

Adrian smirked. "You clean up well, Daisy."

"Thank you," I said. "He bought the dress."

James didn't deny it.

I added sweetly, "I argued."

Adrian laughed outright. "I like her."

Marcus leaned closer to James. "She's already winning."

James rolls his eyes and gently pushes him away, his friends laughing.

Throughout the evening, James stayed... attentive.

Not hovering. Not distant.

He reintroduced me to donors, board members, and politicians. Not as his secretary but as his date. Always with a hand on my back, giving a quiet cue when to step forward, when to disengage. We even danced to a few of the songs when appropriate.

It felt nice. I almost allowed myself to believe it was real. *Almost.*

When the night ended, he accompanied me back home in his limo. The ride was quiet, and the city felt softer somehow.

"You did well," he said eventually.

I give a smile and a small thanks, not knowing how to continue the conversation. Once we arrive, he walks me to my door, both of us walking side by side, enjoying the silence.

"Have a good night, Daisy," He says. "Keep me updated with your cousin's wedding so I can prepare adequately."

"I wi-"

He walks away before I can answer.

What a night.

Thirteen

JAMES

2005

"You sent her this...."

"I did."

"What did she say?"

"She didn't reply."

"Of course she didn't," Marcus scoffs. "Why would you send this?"

I look at Marcus and back at Adrian, who was reading the email I sent to Daisy yesterday morning. And this morning, instead of seeing her, I'm met with Blake letting me know she called off.

She rarely calls off last minute.

I look at the screen, rereading the email, not understanding what was wrong with it.

Ms. Johnson,

Thank you for your work last night.

The Gala proceeded without incident, and several

contacts followed up this morning with positive feedback regarding our presentation and alignment. I consider the evening a success.

Please adjust my schedule for next week to allow a later start on Monday. I will not be taking meetings before noon. If anyone asks, tell them I am reviewing long-term planning initiatives.

Additionally, ensure the dry cleaning receipt is submitted for reimbursement. The dress should be handled carefully. It mattered that it fit properly, and I appreciate that you treated it as such.

We will discuss the next steps later today, during office hours.

As always,

James Wyatt

P.S. There is something I did not anticipate. I do not understand why, but I find it distracting when others refer to you as "Daisy." Please correct this if it occurs again. For clarity, "Daisy" is sufficient.

"What's wrong with it?" I ask, raising a brow.

Marcus laughs under his breath. "It's the ending, man. The 'Daisy' part. You literally made a postscript about a nickname."

Adrian looks up, smirking. "I mean, the rest of the email is professional. Polite. Appreciative. Perfect. But the P.S.? It's... weirdly possessive. But kind of cute."

I frown, not sure whether to be annoyed or amused. "It's a correction. A clarification."

"Yeah, but you don't just drop it in a P.S. like it's an afterthought," Marcus teases. "It's like... 'oh also, don't let anyone else call her Daisy, I can't handle it.'"

Adrian laughs outright. "Exactly. That's the part she'll notice first."

I ignored him and stood, pacing the length of my office. "She called off today. Blake said she left a message early this morning. No explanation. No reply to the email. That's... unlike her."

Marcus raised a brow. "So?"

"So," I continued, "I followed up."

"With what?" Adrian asked cautiously.

I stopped pacing.

"I sent flowers."

Marcus groaned. "Oh no."

"And a gift," I added.

Adrian closed his eyes. "James."

"It was reasonable," I said defensively. "A gesture. Marcus said women appreciate gestures."

"Now, why the fuck would you listen to Marcus?" Adrian snorts, earning exaggerated gasps from the others.

Marcus held up his hands. "I said *thoughtful* gestures. Not... whatever you consider normal."

I turned my screen toward them. The delivery confirmations sat neatly in my inbox.

Flowers. Jewelry. A designer bag I knew she'd never buy for herself. A spa voucher. A book collection, first editions, of an author I'd once seen on her desk.

Silence stretched.

"How many?" Marcus asked quietly.

I hesitated. "Several."

Adrian rubbed his face. "You tried to buy her compliance."

"That is not-"

"That is exactly what you did," Adrian interrupted. "You didn't hear back, so you escalated. Gifts instead of conversation."

Marcus tilted his head. "Did she acknowledge any of it?"

"No."

"And you didn't think," Adrian said slowly, "that maybe something else was going on?"

I stay silent. Not knowing what to say. Not understanding what he meant.

Both take a deep breath, sending a look to each other. Marcus is the first to break the silence.

"Have you heard from the client yet?" He asks, changing the topic. I send him a silent thank you for changing the conversation.

"Yes, they agree to meet, we need to tighten up security before the meeting because I don't want to be in the middle of a war between the Russians and Japanese."

"How were you able to get them in one room?" Adrian asked. "They have been at each other's neck for centuries."

"I can be persuasive." I brush off, not feeling the need to go into details.

I made the risky choice of threatening not to work with either and instead work with the Italians, their enemy, and that quickly got them to agree with my terms. I know if Marcus and Adrian find out, I won't hear the end of it.

You could've gotten yourself killed. Why do something so reckless? They would say.

They wouldn't understand that I don't care. That even if I got killed, it wouldn't matter. It's not like I would be leaving anyone behind.

As night falls and I leave the office, I find myself making my way to Daisy's building. When I reached her door, I noticed the boxes outside.

Untouched.

The flowers were wilting slightly at the edge, ribbon still pristine, packages intact. Nothing brought inside.

My jaw tightens at that, and I knock on her door.

Nothing.

I knock again. Harder this time.

Still silence.

I check my watch. It's early evening. She should still be awake.

I knock a third time, harder, sharper.

"Ms. Johnson," I called through the door. "It's James."

Silence.

I was reaching for my phone, already thinking of who I could call to get access to her place, when I heard it.

Slow. Shuffling.

The lock clicked. The door opens barely a foot.

She stood there wrapped in a blanket, hair in a bonnet, skin paler than usual. Her eyes were glassy, unfocused.

"Oh," she said hoarsely. "Hi."

My irritation vanished instantly.

"You're sick," I state the obvious.

She blinked. "Yes."

"Why didn't you tell anyone?"

"I did," she said, squinting slightly. "I called Blake. Left a message. Did he not... explain?

I shake my head. "You didn't respond to my email."

She frowned. "Email?"

I stared at her.

"I've been asleep most of yesterday and today," she continued weakly. "I only woke up because you kept knocking like the building was on fire."

I looked past her, into the apartment. Curtains drawn. Lights off. Tissues scattered on the coffee table. A half-empty mug near the couch. Medicine bottles on the counter.

I've never seen her space so disorganized.

"I sent you several things," I said slowly.

Her eyes followed mine to the boxes outside the door. Confusion crossed her face.

"...Oh."

"You didn't bring them in."

"I didn't know they were there," she said honestly. "I haven't opened the door since last night."

I exhaled sharply through my nose, something uncomfortable tightening in my chest.

"You should have contacted me directly," I said.

"Why?" She laughed weakly. "You're my boss, not my husband."

The words landed harder than they should have.

I stepped closer, lowering my voice. "You're too sick to be alone."

She swayed slightly. I reacted without thinking, placing a hand on her elbow to steady her.

She didn't pull away.

"Easy," I said.

Her forehead was burning.

"You shouldn't be standing," I added.

"I didn't want to be rude," she murmured. "You kept knocking."

I glanced down the hallway, then back at her. "Go sit."

She hesitated.

"That wasn't a request," I said more gently than I intended.

She shuffled backward, and I followed her inside, closing the door behind me.

Her apartment felt different in daylight. Smaller. More fragile. So was she.

She sank onto the couch, curling into herself.

"I'm sorry," she said quietly. "If I missed something important."

"You didn't," I replied immediately, surprising her.

"I assumed," I continued, choosing my words carefully, "that your silence was intentional."

Her brow furrowed. "Why would you assume that?"

I didn't answer.

She studied me for a moment, then sighed. "James..."

I still, hearing her say my name for the first time. *I think I like it.*

"If I ever don't respond," she continues, not realizing the effect my name coming out of her mouth did to me. "It's not because I'm playing games. I don't do that."

"I know," As I say that, I realized that I actually hadn't known.

I glanced again at the door. "The gifts-"

"Are a lot," she said softly. "But appreciated... thank you."

I stood there awkwardly, unsure what to do next. Fixing problems was easy. This wasn't a problem.

"I'll have someone bring you soup," I said finally.

She rolled her eyes weakly. "Please don't."

"I'm not asking."

She laughed, then coughed. Hard.

I stiffened. "You need rest."

"I know."

Without thinking, I get her a glass of water, holding it as she drinks out of my hand, my other hand drawing comforting circles on her back.

"I'll be fine," she whispers once she finishes, her voice weak. "You can go now. I don't want to get you sick."

I shake my head, taking my phone out and sending a message, "After your soup comes."

With my words, she nods, leaning back into her cocoon on the couch, pressing play on the rom-com she was watching. I keep my eyes on her, not understanding my behavior. If it were anyone else, I would've left and have one of my workers send a care package.

But with Daisy, it's different.

I don't know why. I don't understand why.

But what I do know is that I will stay until she eats her soup and feels better.

Fourteen

DESIREE

2005

My boss is feeding me soup.

And I don't know how to feel about that.

I assumed he would leave after the soup was delivered, but he didn't. Instead, I wake up to him warming up the soup and toasting bread. To which he proceeded to spoon-feed me because I was "too weak" to do it myself.

I'm embarrassed to admit, I didn't put up much of a fight.

It's nice having someone take care of me.

"You don't have to come to the office this week," He says out of nowhere, his brow furrowing in concentration as he makes sure not to drop any soup while feeding me. "Come back when you're fully recovered."

I nod silently, drinking the soup. Once finished, he walks to the kitchen and starts to wash the dirty dishes.

Feeling a bit better, I get up and walk to him, "You don't have to do that."

He shrugs, "I already started, no need to stop now."

"Still," I start to protest, but he doesn't let me.

He points to the chair near the island, "Sit."

I do.

I find myself enamored by his back as he washes the dishes. It was weird to see my boss doing my dishes after taking care of me.

To be honest, it's very hot.

His back is muscular and bulging through his fitted shirt. My eyes drop to his forearm, which is currently flexing as he scrubs the bowl.

Yeah. I lick my suddenly dry lip. *Extremely Hot.*

"Daisy?"

I look up, blinking out of my daze, and I find him standing in front of me. James tilts his head to the side, and I do the same, both of us not breaking eye contact.

It wasn't until his cold hand pressed on my forehead that I remembered who was standing in front of me, "Seems like your fever is getting worse, your face is flushed."

The fever isn't why.

"Oh,"

"You should get some rest. I'll finish everything here."

Why did he even need romance lessons? I ask myself, finding it harder and harder not to swoon.

"You don't have t-"

"I don't mind, I can't stand a messy environment."

My face flushed more, but this time it was more out of embarrassment as I looked around my apartment.

I make my way to my room before he could accidentally insult me further, but stop before entering, looking back at him, "Mr. Wyatt?" I call out.

He stops what he's doing, looking back at me, "James."

"Huh?"

He clears his throat, "You can call me James."

"Oh."

"You were saying, Daisy?"

"Um, just that you would make a good father."

He stiffens at my words, not expecting them. To be honest, I wasn't expecting it either, but now that I've said it, I think it's true.

"I wouldn't." His voice was rigid, as if I had insulted him with that comment. "But thank you, it means a lot coming from you."

Before I could say more, he waved me away, focusing on his task at hand.

Strange.

Fifteen

JAMES

2027

The mall is louder than I remembered.

Not just the sound, but also the movement. Teenagers spilling over each other, kids pulling their parents, and music pulsing faintly from stores to convince you to come in.

Aisha walks two steps ahead of me, already halfway into her favorite clothing store. I offered to buy the store for her, but she said that was "too embarrassing".

Teenagers.

"Don't run," I call as she picks up her pace a bit more. My heart is skipping at the thought of her tripping and hurting herself.

She turns and gives me a sheepish smile, "Do I have a budget?"

I stare at her blankly, trying to figure out if this is one of those teasing moments or if she was serious. She giggles, takes my hand, and pulls me into the store.

As we go through different stores, she hands me the bags, swipes my card without looking at the numbers, and walks away without looking back because she knows I'm behind her. I send a thankful prayer for making her more like her mother than me.

We're in the fifth store when she holds up a jacket, black, oversized, intentionally distressed, and looks at me expectantly.

"What do you think?"

Looks like something her boyfriend would wear.

I study it seriously. "It appears pre-damaged."

"It's fashion," She laughs, putting it in the cart. "Everyone is wearing it now."

"I don't understand."

She shakes her head and pats me on the back, "Mom will explain it, ask her."

I nod, following her as she gets more outfits and little trinkets, "You don't have to move to a dorm, you know? We can get you an apartment near the school, or like a house."

She snorts, "Nope. Not allowed."

I know she's lying, but I say nothing. Daisy mentioned that this is the most important developmental stage of her life, and I need to give her her freedom rather than micromanage.

I tried to explain that Aisha has always been allowed her freedom, staying out late, going to her friend's house, and doing whatever she wants without asking.

But apparently, according to Daisy, secretly tracking her and hacking in peoples/location security systems to watch her every move doesn't count as giving freedom.

So, no more hiding trackers on her phone and car. No hacking cameras. And no, having people go through her data history.

Aisha would kill me if she knew all of this. Even if I assure her that I never looked through the history myself. I just want to make sure she's safe.

But because of Daisy's new rules, I cannot help but feel a sense of unease. The idea of my little girl not being under my watch doesn't feel right. What if she doesn't keep track of her doctor's appointment, what if she meets another man like Anthony... what if.... what if...*what if?*

"Daddy?"

"Huh?"

"I said, there's one your size, do you want to match?"

I hesitate a bit, looking at the distress material and into my daughter's eyes before giving a nod, "I'd love that."

We end up at a café in the center of the mall, bags at our feet, drinks sweating onto the table. I watch Aisha as she scrolls through her phone, straw between her lips.

I don't watch her in the way I used to, scanning for danger, calculating outcomes. I just... watch. Observing who she's become.

Confident. Intelligent. Beautiful.

"Aisha," I say.

She hums in response, eyes still on the screen.

"I need to apologize to you."

She looks up immediately. "...Again?" she asks gently.

"Yes," I say. "Again."

She sets her phone down and gives me a silent gesture to continue.

I take a deep breath.

"I've apologized before for what I said. For minimizing your boyfriend. For being absent." I pause. "But I don't think I ever fully apologized for *why* I said it."

Her expression tightens, but she doesn't interrupt.

"I was wrong," I continue. "Not because I was afraid for you, that part was real. But because I believed my fear gave me the right to override your love. Your agency."

I look down at my hands. Old habit. Then force myself to meet her eyes.

"I treated you like something fragile I needed to control

instead of a person who had already survived things I couldn't imagine."

She swallows.

"I know I was absent," I say quietly. "Physically. Emotionally. I hid behind work, behind money, behind your mother's strength. And when you found someone who showed up for you in ways I hadn't..." My voice tightens. "I lashed out."

She's very still now.

"I didn't just insult him," I say. "I dismissed the fact that he loved you the way you needed. That's not protection. That's my ego."

Silence stretches between us. The noise of the mall fades into background static. Finally, she speaks. "You know," she starts slowly, "that wasn't the worst part."

I nod. "I know."

"The worst part," she continues, "was thinking that if I chose him, if I chose *myself,* I was losing you."

My chest tightens.

"And that," she adds, "wasn't fair either."

"I know," I say again. Softer this time. "I'm sorry I made love feel conditional."

Her eyes glisten, but she doesn't cry. Lately, I've noticed that Aisha doesn't cry much around me anymore. That revelation should break my heart, but it doesn't.

Best if she doesn't depend on me for emotional support.

"You've been better," she admits. "You try. You show up. You listen... most of the time."

"I'm still learning," I say. "I spent years believing love was something you managed, not something you practiced."

She tilts her head. "Mom taught you that?"

I smile faintly. "Amongst other things."

She studies me for a moment, then reaches across the table and nudges my wrist with her fingers.

"You don't have to keep apologizing forever," she says. "Just don't stop being different."

"I won't," I promise. And for once, I mean it without conditions.

She stands, grabbing her drink. "Come on. We still need shoes."

I rise, collecting the bags again.

As we walk, she glances at me sideways.

"For what it's worth," she says, "you were right about one thing back then."

"Oh?" I ask warily.

"He *is* a little obsessed with me."

I huff a quiet laugh. "I noticed."

She smiles before already weaving back into the crowd.

I follow, carrying the weight gladly.

Daisy will be proud.

DESIREE

2005

As the driver gets closer to the wedding venue, I wonder if it's not too late to cancel and admit my lie.

When I told my aunt I would be bringing someone, I forgot my parents and siblings would also be attending the wedding.

My parents and I had a silent agreement to avoid any contact with each other. The only person in my family that I talk to is my older siblings, but with our age gap and the fact that they have their own families, we rarely see each other.

Plus, they had the privilege of leaving my parents before they started to get worse.

"Daisy?"

I turn to James, his voice pulling me out of my thoughts, "Huh?"

"Are you okay?" His voice is still monotoned, but the more I get to know him, I feel as if I can understand his underlying emotions.

Right now, he's concerned. I can tell that with the way his eyes move frantically around my face, he only does that when he is trying to read my expressions.

I give him a big smile, "Yeah, just nervous... my family can be difficult."

He tilts his head in confusion, "And that's a problem because?"

I take a deep breath, a bit frustrated that he doesn't understand, but when I see the oblivious look on his face, that quickly fades away.

"Imagine how the Whitlock makes you feel," His face scrunches into a frown. "That's how they make me feel."

He nods, "Oh."

"Yeah."

"So you want them to die?" He says while pulling out his phone to type something.

My eyebrows shot up in surprise, "N-no, no," I waved my hand in panic. "That is not what I mean."

At my words, he puts his phone away. I try not to think about what that small action meant, "So what do you want?"

"I don't know," I admit. "I just... don't want them in my life anymore."

"And is that not the same as wanting them to die?"

I try not to focus on the fact that I found his confusion kind of adorable because that would also mean admitting that something is wrong with me.

"It's different," I start. "Because I don't want them to leave the earth, I just want them to leave me alone."

"Why?"

"Because they are a bunch of lowlife hypocrites who deserve all the bad luck coming to them." I seethe, remembering how they hurt me. How they chose to support an outsider and not their own flesh and blood.

James laugh brings me out of my thoughts. I try not to act

surprised, but fail when I see tears fall out of his eyes. *Did I miss something?*

"I'm sorry," He says, wiping away a tear. "I don't think your situation is funny, but your angry face is adorable. You look like a bloodthirsty bunny."

"I-" I don't know what to say. He keeps laughing, it's a throaty laugh, like something he doesn't do often. I find myself joining him, not being able to stop.

We laugh for what seems like forever until we pull up at the wedding venue. We stand in front of the car, not a few people present in the venue since we arrived earlier than usual.

I didn't want to bring attention by arriving fashionably late.

He extends his arm out to me, and I take it, anchoring myself. "Let's get this over with," I smile up at him.

"Relax," He says, "It won't be that bad."

When did he become so optimistic?

Coming late and sitting in the back corner, away from my parents and siblings, did not help my case. It didn't help having James Wyatt sitting next to me, in an immaculate tailored suit and magnifying aura.

I made brief eye contact with my parents when they first walked in. My dad quickly avoided my gaze while my mom kept staring, itching to come over to talk to James.

Some of my cousins and distant family members came by and gave a small polite greeting and introduced themselves to James. My aunt, Lorraine, being the mother of the bride, couldn't come to talk, but she did give me a *We'll talk later* look across the venue.

Once the ceremony ended, we all made our way to another hall for the reception. I stopped a few times by family friends, all wanting to know more about James.

The reception hall is loud, buzzing with gossip and laughter as everyone catches up with each other while finding their assigned seats.

James stays by my side quietly, his hands brushing mine occasionally as I read the sitting chart. I cringed when I saw where I was sitting. It was a given since no one outside the household knows what happened.

"Come," I say to James. "Let's get this over with."

We make our way to our seats, walking hand in hand, when my aunt spots us midway.

"Desiree!"

She's on me in seconds, arms pulling me into a tight hug that smells like hairspray and floral perfume. Her eyes flick immediately to James.

"Well, I'll be," she says, pulling back. "You *did* bring someone."

Here we go.

"This is James," I say, keeping my tone even. "James Wyatt."

He steps forward smoothly, offering his hand. "It's a pleasure to finally meet you."

My aunt's eyebrows lift. "Well, aren't you handsome," she says, shaking his hand. "And polite. Lord, Desiree, where have you been hiding him?"

"I wasn't hiding," I mutter.

James smiles and says nothing.

"Well, why don't you and your beau go and have a seat, dear," She smiles, giving me a teasing wink. "Being the mother of the bride comes with endless duties; we'll talk later."

By the time we made it to the table, my parents, siblings, and *him* were already eyeing us. As James pulls a chair for me to sit, Lauren clears her throat, "So, Desiree...." She purrs. "Gonna introduce us to your new *friend?*"

"Why so you could fuck this one too?" Marie, my sister younger than me by a year, whispers under her breath. My dad coughs awkwardly.

"Marie Johnson, watch your language," Mom scowls. "We are in the presence of company. I raised you better than that."

Marie smirks, "You also raised me to always be honest."

Before they could start a back and forth, my dad spoke, "What's your name, young man?"

"James Wyatt."

The table goes quiet, no doubt realizing who was sitting at the table with them. My eyes fell to *him* without meaning to, finding that he was already looking at me, trying to catch my eyes.

I ignored, planting a fake smile and looking up at James, who was engaged in small talk with my family.

"I'm happy that Daisy found someone of your stature. She has made some questionable decisions in her past," Mom comments, so full of herself she doesn't even realize she just insulted her son-in-law.

I look back at *him* again, his eyes cast down in embarrassment. Lauren shifting uncomfortably next to him.

Him being JJ.

My good-for-nothing ex, whom my family once hated, is now married to my youngest sister, fathering her children.

"How did you get Desiree to be with you?" Mom continues, "She tends to go after the broken things, the losers, not someone as successful as you?"

"Mom's right, sis," Marie teases, sending a wink at JJ, who is trying to make himself invisible. "You deserve better than the mess you had in the past."

"Marie..." Lauren warns, face red in embarrassment. "Watch your mouth."

"What?" She fakes innocence. "I'm just agreeing with mom."

"Daisy is a smart, capable, beautiful woman," James says calmly, cutting through the tension. "And anyone who's had the privilege of being with her should consider themselves fortunate, regardless of how it ended."

The table goes quiet.

I look at him, surprised.

My mom clears her throat. "Well... that's one way to put it."

"Where's Carol and the others?" I ask, wanting to change the conversation.

"Your sister's flight was delayed, so she'll be late. As for Robert, Joshua, Crystal, and Isaiah, I have no idea." Dad answers vaguely, but we all know that's a lie.

My sibling just didn't care to be around my parents and Lauren.

"How many siblings do you have?" James whispers in my ear.

"Seven," I whisper back. "Carol, Isaiah, and Crystal are older than I, and Marie, Joshua, Robert, and Lauren are younger."

"Do you have a big family, James?" Lauren asks, seeming to finally find her voice after the way Mom embarrassed her.

"No," He says curtly. "I'm the only child, so were my parents, and my grandparents."

"Must be a lonely life, I can't imagine not having siblings."

Both Marie and I scoff at her words. *Of course, the spoiled baby would think that.*

"I want a big family," She continues, ignoring us. "That's why JJ and I are about to have our third one this year."

My parents gasp in shock while my eyes bulge out of my head. Lauren smirks, rubbing her abdomen, "We wanted to keep it a secret, but I just couldn't."

"Three under two, those poor nannies," Marie comments. "Congratulations to the happy couple."

"Yeah," I bite my inner cheek to restrain my words. "Congratulations."

Seventeen

JAMES

2005

I don't like weddings. Or any social gatherings for that matter.

I think they are inefficient, loud, and emotionally excessive. And yet, I'm in one.

The reception hall is glowing in warm gold light, chandeliers dimmed just enough to make everything feel softer than it is. Music pulses through the room, the dance floor is crowded, heels abandoned near tables, ties loosened, jackets draped over chairs.

And Daisy...

Daisy is drunk.

Ever since her sister announced her pregnancy, she has been drinking nonstop. But she wasn't sloppy or reckless, just bright.

Her laughter carries over the music as she spins with one of her cousins, her dress catching the light. Her hair, which she had pinned neatly for the ceremony, is now wild around her shoulders.

I stand near the bar, nursing my whiskey and observing her.

Her family left an hour ago, and the change in her behavior astonished me. I figured she would want to leave, but she mentioned wanting to see her older sister, Carol, first.

Who is still running late.

"Why aren't you dancing?"

I glance to my right.

A woman stands beside me, tall, poised, dressed in deep emerald silk that hugs her frame like it was sewn onto her. Her posture is confident, chin lifted slightly, eyes sharp.

She looks like Daisy but more *polished.*

"Carol," I say.

Her lips curve. "So she talks about me."

"Not really," I bluntly let out. "But I've already met Marie and Lauren, and was told Crystal wasn't attending."

Her eyes narrow to slits at me. I quickly remember Daisy warning me that blunt honesty isn't always a good thing.

"She did say you are her favorite," I soften the blow, and to that she smiles.

"You're a clever one."

I say nothing, instead I let her study me openly. A part of me wants to make a good impression on Daisy's favorite sister.

"You're quieter than I expected," she finally says.

"You're later than I expected," I reply.

She laughs, low and pleased. 'Touché."

We watch Daisy for a moment. She was now attempting to teach an elderly aunt a line dance. It's not going well.

"It's been a while since she had fun like this," Carol says softly.

I look at her.

"Ever since JJ," Carol continues. "She never had fun with the family like this. It's nice."

"What did JJ do?"

Carol turns to me slowly. "She hasn't told you?"

I shake my head. She nods understandingly, "She will eventually."

Across the room, Daisy finally notices us.

Her eyes widen.

"Oh no," Carol mutters under her breath with a small laugh. "She sees us."

Daisy weaves through guests with the determined focus of someone operating at ten percent sobriety.

"CAROL!" She yells, unnecessarily loud.

Carol opens her arms just in time before Daisy crashes into her.

"You're late," Daisy accuses, words slightly slurred.

"I'm fashionably late," Carol corrects. "There's a difference."

Daisy pulls back and looks between us suspiciously. "Are you interrogating him?"

"Yes," Carol says calmly.

"No," I say at the same time.

Daisy gasps. "You're ganging up on me."

Carol rolls her eyes. "You're drunk."

"I am festive," Daisy corrects.

I feel something unfamiliar tug at my mouth.

Amusement.

"Why?" Carol continues her interrogation.

Daisy's smile falters a little before it's back on her face, "Well, haven't you heard? Our dearest sister is pregnant with her third."

"Oh Desiree..."

"Yup," Daisy continues. "My ex-boyfriend and the sister he cheated on me with are having their third baby."

That information surprises me. From what I saw earlier, I assumed tension was high, but I did not realize it was that horrid.

"He doesn't deserve your self-pity," I commented before I could realize.

Daisy turns to me suddenly, gripping my suit jacket with both hands and flashing me one of her dazzling smiles.

"Are you having fun?" She demands.

"Yes."

"Are you lying?"

"I have never lied to you, Daisy."

"On a scale of one to ten?"

"Seven."

Her eyes narrow. "Seven is a low score."

"It's above average."

She stares at me for a long moment before nodding in acceptance, "Okay."

Carol looks between us again, expression unreadable.

"So," she says lightly, "Is your family as dysfunctional as ours?"

"I don't have a family," I answer bluntly.

"Maybe that's a good thing," Daisy mumbles, her face on the crook of my neck, using me as a crutch. "Less mess to deal with."

"Now hush you," Carol scold at her sister before bringing her attention to me. "You're coming to Thanksgiving."

I blink once. Daisy's grip on my jacket tightens slightly.

"That was not a question," Carol adds.

Daisy gasps dramatically. "Yes! Yes, you have to come!"

"I don't *have* to do anything," I say evenly.

Daisy leans closer, eyes wide and sparkling with alcohol and something softer.

"You do," she whispers loudly. "You don't get to be alone on holidays."

"That sounds like a rule you just invented."

"It is," she says proudly.

Carol folds her arms. "We're loud. We have drama. We always argue. But we show up."

Daisy nods vigorously. "We show up."

"And," Carol continues. "*That* part of the family won't be present; they stopped attending years ago."

I look at Daisy, cheeks flushed, smile unguarded, eyes hopeful. The logical part of me wants to remind her that this wedding is the end of our agreement, that come tomorrow, we don't have to pretend.

But as she relaxes into me, I find myself not listening to my logical side for the first time. "Fine,"

She squeals while Carol smiles like she just closed a negotiation.

"But," I add, "I'm not going around saying what I'm thankful for."

Carol laughs. "We'll negotiate."

Daisy beams up at me like I've given her the world.

"You're going to love it," she promises.

I doubt that.

But as she leans her head briefly against my chest, content and warm and unafraid-

I realize something unsettling.

I am already looking forward to it.

Across the room, someone calls Daisy's name for another dance.

She pulls away, pointing at me dramatically.

"Don't leave!"

"I won't," I say.

She hesitates, then runs back to the dance floor.

Eighteen

DESIREE

2005

Carol's house smells like butter, garlic, and something burning.

"Nothing's burning," she yells from the kitchen before I fully step inside.

"I didn't say anything!" I call back.

"You didn't have to!"

I grin and slip off my coat.

James closes the door behind us with quiet precision, like Carol's suburban split-level might collapse if he shuts it too hard.

It's been two weeks since the wedding, and James has been away for work. Our communication is limited to formal emails.

I assumed he backed out of the invitation, but yesterday he showed up at my door with his suitcase packed, upgraded my plane tickets, and got himself a seat next to mine.

And now, we're across the country at Carol's. With her husband Jeremy, her kids, my brothers, and sisters (minus Lauren).

My nephew, Joseph, is the first to run over to greet us, "Hi, Auntie, did you bring me a gift?"

I laugh, picking him up into a hug and slipping some cash in his hands, "Don't tell you, mom." I whisper.

Jeremy is next to follow, giving me a big hug, almost lifting me off the ground. "How are you, little sis?"

I pat his back, wheezing as he squeezes me, "I... can't... breathe."

He drops me immediately. "Sorry. Sorry."

"You say that every time," Carol calls from the kitchen. "And yet."

James stands a step behind me, hands loosely clasped in front of him, observing the chaos like it's a live case study.

Joseph finally notices him.

"...Who's that?" he whispers loudly.

I glance back. James looks perfectly composed in a charcoal sweater and dark slacks, like he's attending a board meeting instead of Thanksgiving in suburbia.

"This is James," I say. "He's my—"

There's a microscopic pause.

My what?

Boss? Date?

"Friend," I finish.

James' eyes flick to me briefly. Neutral. Unreadable.

Joseph squints at him. "Are you rich?"

"Joseph!" Carol snaps from the kitchen.

James doesn't miss a beat. "Extremely."

Jeremy bursts out laughing. "I like him already."

Joseph studies him for another second. "Did you bring me a gift too?"

James crouches down so they're eye level. "I was informed monetary contributions were preferred."

Joseph's eyes widen. "You gave me money?!"

"I did not say that," James replies calmly.

Joseph runs off to count his cash anyway.

Jeremy shakes his head. "You're fitting in just fine, man."

James stands again, smoothing an invisible wrinkle from his sleeve. "Thanks."

The house is loud. Kids chasing each other. Football on TV. Some are arguing about a show.

James sits still next to me in the living room. We're watching the game while we wait for the food to be ready. Carol refused to have anyone go into her kitchen.

"You okay?" I murmur, stepping closer.

"Yes," he says immediately.

"You look like you're about to audit the furniture."

"I'm just observing," he replies.

"Of course you are."

Carol appears from the kitchen, wooden spoon in hand like a weapon. "James Wyatt," she says, eyeing him. "You're chopping vegetables."

He blinks once. "Am I?"

"Yes."

He looks at me. I blink back.

"I thought no one was allowed in her kitchen?" He whispers to me in urgency.

I smile sympathetically before whispering back, "I think she's testing you."

Carol grins triumphantly and disappears back into the kitchen.

James exhales through his nose. "This is coercion."

But he follows Carol to the kitchen. I watch him chop the carrots with surgical precision, his suit jacket now off, and his dress shirt rolled up.

Crystal plops down next to me, wiggling her brow at me, "Marie told me your new beau was fly, I didn't expect him to be this fine."

Robert sits on my opposite side, both siblings squeezing me in, "At first, I wasn't for you dating your boss. But I got a good feeling about this one."

I feel my heart turn at his words, the small bliss I felt immediately gone. James is my *boss.* This is *fake.*

I try to remind myself, but as I watch him chop the vegetables and follow Carol's orders, I decide to stay in that bliss.

Robert, my youngest brother, enters the kitchen, leaning against the counter. "You cook?"

"I can follow instructions."

"That's more than most men," Roberts mutters, earning a huge laugh out of us.

I get up and hover near the doorway, pretending like I'm not staring.

"Do you need any help, sis?"

Carol rolls her eyes, "Come help your boyfriend since you apparently can't stay away from him for long."

I blush in embarrassment. James glances up as I get closer, and our eyes meet. There's something softer there than usual. Something less calculated.

Joseph runs back in, making us break eye contact, "Uncle James-"

The room goes quiet.

James stills mid-slice. Carol's eyebrows shoot up, and Jeremy coughs to hide a laugh.

I feel more heat rush to my face.

Joseph looks confused. "What? That's what you call the guy who comes to Thanksgiving with Auntie."

James slowly sets the knife down.

He turns to Joseph calmly. "You may call me James."

Joseph nods. "Okay, Uncle James."

Jeremy loses it, laughing openly now.

Carol wipes her hands on a towel, smirking. "Guess it's settled."

I can't look at him. I can feel him looking at me.

I just rushed out of the room ignoring the teasing from my siblings.

Once dinner rolls around, everyone is in good spirits, the kids are playing and eating, majority of the adults are a bit buzzy from wine and having a good time.

James and I sat together; he was silent, observing everything and eating while I listened to Isaiah telling me about the funny thing his youngest daughter did the other day.

Midway through dinner, Carol taps her glass. "Okay! Time for gratitude circle!"

James' posture stiffens instantly.

I bite back a laugh.

"Absolutely not," he mutters under his breath.

"Too late," Crystal grins. "You're at the end of the table. You're going last."

One by one, everyone shares something they're thankful for.

Health. Jobs. Babies.

When it gets to me, I hesitate. I wasn't planning to say anything serious.

But my eyes drift to him.

"I'm thankful," I say slowly, "for people who show up when they don't have to."

The table hums softly. Next, it was his turn; he cleared his throat once, shifting a bit uncomfortably.

"I'm thankful," he says evenly, "for those who make everyone feel a sense of belonging."

The table smiles at that.

The feeling in my chest roars, and I'm unable to hide the storm brewing inside.

I'm crushing on my boss.

DESIREE

2005

After dinner, when the dishes are done and the kids are asleep, I step outside onto the porch for air.

The night is cold and quiet

A minute later, the door opens behind me. I don't need to turn to know exactly who it was.

"You had fun," I say.

"Yes."

"Scale of one to ten?"

He considers it.

"Eight."

I grin. "That's an improvement."

"Yes."

We stand side by side, no touching, just...close.

"Thank you," I say quietly.

"For what?"

"For coming."

He looks at me then, "You didn't want me to be alone," he says.

"No, I didn't."

"So I should be thanking you, not the other way around."

I smile at that, and both of us turn to watch the stars in silence. Enjoying each other's company.

After a while, he is the first to break the silence, "Daisy-"

"Why do you call me that?" I interrupt.

"Huh?"

"Why do you call me Daisy?"

He blinks, a look of confusion on his face, "Do you not remember?" He asks.

Now it's my turn to be confused, "Remember what?"

"When you first started working in the company," He speaks slowly, cautiously. "You always used to have daisies on your nails."

A memory flashes back to me. I look at my nails, which are currently sporting a simple French tip polish.

I haven't had fun nails since the big fight with my family three years ago.

"You're childish, always with these hopes and dreams. Look at your nails, your room, your hair.

"God, Desiree, when will you ever grow up?"

"No wonder he left you for Lauren."

"I'll be honest," His voice brings me out of my mind. He's rubbing the back of his neck in embarrassment. "Once I forgot your first name, but I saw that daisy on your nail, and I guess that just stuck."

I laugh at his words, the hurtful feeling from my memory disappearing. "I figured that was a part of it."

"Do you hate it?"

I hesitate before shaking my head, "I used to when I thought it was because you didn't care to learn my name, but I don't anymore."

"Is that why you threw away the flowers I gave you?"

"What do you mean? I took care of the bouquet you sent when I was sick."

He shakes his head, "No, not those."

"Then what?"

When has he ever sent me flowers aside from the day I was sick?

"The ones I sent you on your anniversary at the company, I noticed them in the trash."

I freeze.

"*You* sent those two bouquets?"

He shakes his head, "No, just the one. For your first year in the company, I sent Gardenias to show you how proud I was of your growth in the company, and you looked very happy to receive them."

I feel myself getting dizzy with his words. I remember that bouquet; it was the most beautiful bouquet. The note read.

Happy First Anniversary at this company! You have worked so hard, and I'm proud of your growth.

I thought those flowers were from JJ, because the night before, I was going on and on about how proud I was of my hard work. I was drunk and complained that my *boss* was probably not even going to congratulate me.

When I saw the flowers, I was so happy that I sent JJ a thank-you paragraph, and that jerk just took the credit.

"So I tried sending it again the following year, but you gave them away to Lucy."

God, I'm going to faint.

I got home early that day, still happy from the flowers, I decided to surprise JJ, and lo and behold. I walked in on him and my sister fucking.

The following year, I got two bouquets, the gardenias and roses. The note on the roses read.

You're invited to Lauren and JJ's baby shower. Let's forget about the past. - Mom & Dad

That led to the big fight. I gave away both bouquets without even bothering to read the second note.

"Marcus said that maybe you were getting tired of the same thing, so I decided to switch it yearly, but you just throw them away every time."

The third year, it was lilies and roses. No notes on the lilies, but the roses were a note from JJ asking for forgiveness. He wanted to meet up for a date and wanted me to be his mistress.

After that, I just stopped reading the notes

"I need to sit down," I mumble, walking to the bench that was on the porch, my mind in turmoil.

He's next to me within seconds, "Are you okay?"

I look at James. His face scrunched up in concern as he examined my face, "You look pale."

"I-," my eyes sting with tears. "I'm sorry."

The dam breaks. I find myself sobbing nonstop, not able to talk. I feel James pacing around me in panic, his arms flying to my face, trying to get my attention.

"H-hey, hey," His voice rings panicky. "It's okay, it's not that big of a deal. *Please* stop crying."

If I weren't feeling like a bitch, I would focus on the fact that for the first time, I heard emotions in his voice.

"I-," I hiccup. "I just feel like such an ungrateful bitch, I didn't know."

The number of times I've called him a bad boss.

"Daisy, you're killing me. Please, what can I do to make you stop crying?" He begs, wiping away my tears.

I blame my emotional state for what I do next. Looking down at James, who was kneeling in front of me, I threw myself on him and hugged him.

My actions shock him at first, but at my next sniffle, he hugs me back. I feel him shift for a bit, picking me up and sitting on the bench while I cry on his lap.

I'm going to regret this tomorrow, but as I felt the muscles on his chest and his strong hold as he drew soft circles on my back, I let myself enjoy the moment.

Twenty

JAMES

2005

December settles into a routine. I like routine.

Routine means predictability.

Predictability means control.

Control means nothing goes wrong.

Every morning, Daisy arrives between 8:40-8:50 a.m. She stops by reception first, exchanges pleasantries, collects the day's reports, and then walks into her office carrying coffee she insists tastes better from the cafe across the street.

It does not. But I don't argue.

By 9:00, my schedule is finalized.

By 9:15, she knocks once before entering.

"Good Morning, Mr. Wya- James," she corrects herself. The first time she used my name at work, Blake nearly dropped a folder.

I pretended not to notice the effect it had on me.

Her voice has changed since Thanksgiving. Softer and less guarded. She lingers longer when delivering reports. I find reasons to call her into my office, and our conversations drift away from work more often than they should.

The weather.

Her siblings.

And a rom-com she recommended.

I know more about Daisy Johnson's daily habits than any employer reasonably should.

And she knows when I haven't slept.

"You're doing that thing again," she says one afternoon, setting files on my desk.

"What thing?"

"Staring at spreadsheets like they personally offended you."

I look up.

She smiles.

My chest tightens in a way I am beginning to recognize as dangerous.

My office overlooks hers through reinforced glass.

Officially, it exists for operational oversight.

Unofficially-

The security feed remains open on my secondary monitor at all times.

Camera three shows her desk.

She hums when she works. Quietly. Absentmindedly.

Today it's off-key.

She spins slightly in her chair while typing.

I tell myself I monitor the feed for safety reasons.

The company has enemies. I have enemies.

Association with me carries risk.

This is a precaution.

Nothing more.

"You're doing it again."

Marcus' voice comes from behind me.

I don't turn.

"I'm monitoring company property."

Adrian walks in beside him, already grinning. "Company property has a name."

I finally glance at them. "If you came here to waste my time-"

Marcus leans against the desk, arms crossed. "You've been staring at that camera feed for twelve minutes."

"Thirteen," Adrian corrects. "I timed him."

I mute the screen.

Neither of them looks convinced, but they don't judge, because that would be hypocritical.

Our mortality tends to be flexible.

Our business requires that.

Officially, I work in security consulting, Adrain in International negotiations, and Marcus is in Asset management.

Unofficially, we mediate conflicts that people prefer remain undocumented.

Crime families.

Private syndicates.

And hypocritical governments.

"So," Adrian says casually, picking up a paperweight from my desk. "When were you planning to tell us you're spiraling over your assistant?"

"I am not spiraling."

Marcus gestures toward the blank monitor. "You installed direct office feeds routed privately to your system."

"That was for efficiency."

"You adjusted camera angles," Adrian adds.

Silence.

Marcus whistles low. "Jesus. You adjusted angles."

"It improves visibility."

"Of her desk," Adrian says.

"Yes."

They stare at me.

I stare back.

Marcus finally laughs. "You're gone."

I ignore him and return to my laptop.

A different screen waits there.

Blueprints.

Street layouts.

Fiber access points.

Daisy's apartment building sits centered on the display.

Adrian notices immediately.

"...James."

"Crime statistics indicate elevated risk after dark,"I say calmly.

Marcus rubs his face. "Tell me you're not about to hack residential surveillance."

"I haven't decided."

Adrian snorts. "You already mapped access nodes. You decided."

I pause.

Because the truth is simple.

She lives alone and needs to be protected.

"She's fine," Marcus says, though there's no judgment in his tone.

"I know."

Adrian raises a brow. "Then why?"

The answer forms before I can stop it, "Because knowing isn't the same as verifying."

Both men go quiet for a bit.

Marcus nods slowly, "Yeah, makes sense."

A soft knock sounds through the intercom.

Once.

My attention snaps instantly toward the door as I quickly exit my tab.

Daisy steps inside moments later, unaware she has just ended a criminal ethics discussion.

"I finalized tomorrow's briefing," she says, setting files down. "Also, you skipped lunch again."

"I wasn't hungry."

She narrows her eyes.

"You say that every day."

She moves closer, adjusting my tie without thinking.

The gesture freezes something inside my chest.

Marcus makes a choking noise.

Daisy startles slightly, realizing we're not alone. "Oh, hi, Mr. Hale, Mr. Cole."

Adrian smiles warmly, "Ms. Johnson."

Marcus waves, giving me a knowing look.

Her gaze shifts between us suspiciously, "I'm almost afraid to ask."

"You should be," Adrian says.

I stand immediately. "We're finished here."

We aren't, but they understand dismissal when they hear it.

Adrian pats my shoulder on the way out, "Try not to commit any felonies."

Marcus adds, "Or do. Just loop us in."

They walk out. Daisy looks at me curiously.

She hums, unconvinced.

Then smiles.

And for reasons I cannot logically justify, that smile settles something restless inside me.

She turns to leave.

I watch until she disappears back into her office.

A moment later, the security monitor flickers back on.

Camera 3.

She sits down, tucking her hair behind her ear as she resumes work.

My hand hovers over the keyboard.

After a brief hesitation, I save the apartment surveillance plans anyway.

Just in case.

Routine, after all, requires maintenance.

And Desiree Johnson has quietly become the most important variable in mine.

Twenty-One

DESIREE

2005

Mr. Moreau's brunch is the kind of event where even the sunlight feels curated. Soft piano filters through the hidden speakers. Crystal glasses clink gently. Women dressed in silk, and men in tailored suits.

I smooth over my dress for the fifth time this hour.

"You're doing it again," James murmurs beside me.

"Doing what?"

"Fidgeting."

"I am not."

"You are."

I glare at him. He looks perfectly composed in a dark winter suit, one hand resting lightly at the small of my back as we move through the room. The touch is subtle, yet it sends heat through my body.

We're still "fake dating", none of us brought up ending it or the fact that it was ever fake. Because frankly, ever since Thanksgiving, since the porch, it doesn't feel fake.

At least not to me.

Mr. Moreau greets us with theatrical warmth, walking towards James and me with his wife and daughter on his side.

"Wyatt! You made it."

"Of course," James replies smoothly. "Thank you for the invitation."

"I must say, James," Moreau's gaze shifts to me, eyes twinkling with approval, "I am happy to see you in such a beautiful partnership, especially with someone like Ms. Johnson. She has always been my favorite of your secretaries."

James's hand tightens around my waist. A quiet grumble leaves him, one I'm certain only I hear.

I give Mr. Moreau a soft smile. "Thank you."

The two continue their conversation about contracts and interests while my eyes scan the area until it falls on her.

She stands near the mimosa bar in pale blue, perfectly styled hair, and elegant posture. She looks the same as always, polished and inviting.

Elizabeth.

She notices us. Her eyes furrow in confusion before a wide, graceful smile replaces them.

"James. Mr. Moreau," she says, stepping forward easily. Then her gaze lands on me. "Desiree."

"Hi, Elizabeth."

Her gaze flickers between us, to his hand at my back, to the space we're not leaving between us.

"Oh," she says softly. "You two are together."

James' expression doesn't change. "Yes."

Elizabeth studies him.

Then me.

"You make quite a pair," she says pleasantly. "If you'll excuse me."

She disappears into the crowd.

Once she's out of sight, I look up at James. He's already looking down at me.

"That was awkward."

He tilts his head slightly. "It was?"

I shake mine. "Forget it."

James shrugs, not pressing it any further.

We continue mingling. Well, James does the mingling. I stand beside him, nodding and contributing when necessary. He includes me in conversations every chance he gets, never speaking over me, never dismissing me. It's... nice.

I grew up around social scenes like this, but the way James treats me is completely different from how my parents treated each other.

One of the main reasons my parents and I didn't get along, and why I didn't go to college, was that I refused to live that kind of life.

I was never top of my class. Just adequate. And when it came time for higher education, my parents gave me an ultimatum: marry the son of a business partner, and they would pay for my schooling, or figure it out on my own.

I figured it out on my own.

And I don't regret it.

"Are you ready to go?"

A shiver runs down my spine as James leans close, his voice low against my ear. We're currently listening to Mr. Quinn ramble about a potential partnership. It's taking everything in me not to roll my eyes.

"Let me make a quick trip to the bathroom first," I whisper back.

He nods once, his hand brushing my waist before I step away. I give him and Mr. Quinn a polite smile before slipping into the crowd.

As I walk toward the hallway, I can still feel the warmth of his hand lingering on my back.

And I don't know if that's part of the act anymore.

But I'm starting to hope it isn't.

The bathroom is quieter than the rest of the house. It had soft lighting and marble counters. Two women were currently fixing their lipstick in the mirror. Someone is laughing on the phone.

I move to the sink to wash my hands. The door opens behind me.

"Desiree," Elizabeth steps in, her tone polite and neutral.

I meet her eyes in the mirror. "Elizabeth."

With one look from her, the other women filter out slowly. The room grows quieter.

She walks to the sink beside mine, washing her hands delicately as if this is just another mundane social interaction.

"You look lovely," she says.

"Thank you."

A pause.

"You've always had good taste," she continues. "Anytime I saw you, I was always in awe of your attire."

I don't know what that meant, so I don't respond.

She dries her hands carefully before turning to face me fully.

"I hope you don't mind me being direct," she says.

I already don't like where this is going.

"James and I dated for quite some time in the past."

I nod once. "I'm aware."

She gives a small smile, "He also asked me to marry him before I ended it."

I don't say anything at first because I was the one who picked the engagement ring, "Your point is...."

She pauses for a moment, "James, he doesn't do anything without a reason."

The words settle strangely, even though I knew that.

"He's very strategic," she continues. "Even socially."

"I know that," I straighten slightly. "What are you implying?"

"I'm not implying anything," She tilts her head. "I'm just stating a fact."

I say nothing, she lets out a big sigh.

"One of the biggest reasons why I broke up with James was not just because he was emotionally distant," she says gently. "It's also because I felt like a pawn. I was the logical choice, an asset. Someone he could bring to events that benefit him."

"You benefited too." I point out.

She laughs humorlessly, "Look, Desiree. I like you, you always treated me with kindness and never viewed me as a gold digger."

"Thank you?" My voice is quiet and confused.

"I just want to spread your kindness with a warning," she continues. "If James is here with you, if he's bringing you to events like this... It's because it benefits him."

"That's a stretch."

Denial.

"Is it?" Her gaze sharpens slightly. "Mr. Moreau just publicly praised your 'partnership.' Investors notice stability. Clients prefer it. A grounded executive is a safer executive."

I hate that part of me that understands what she's saying.

"He and I were engaged," she adds. "He respected me. Valued me. But love?" She shakes her head lightly. "James doesn't operate from love."

My throat feels dry, because I knew that was true. The start of this fake relationship was to help me get my family off my back while also teaching him how to love.

I knew James didn't understand love, but he wanted to learn. He wanted to learn to find a wife.

And he's changed so much, became more mindful. Surely what I think he feels for me isn't all fake.

Right?

"You're a sweet girl," she says. "And I would hate for you to misunderstand the nature of what this is."

"And what is this?" I ask before I can stop myself.

She studies me carefully.

"A mutually beneficial arrangement."

The word arrangement echoes unpleasantly.

"He cares about you," she clarifies smoothly. "In his way. You're competent. Loyal. Discreet. You make him look... human."

I feel myself getting numb.

Elizabeth straightens, smoothing imaginary wrinkles from her dress.

"You deserve someone who chooses you for you," she says. "Not because it's convenient."

Convenient.

The word lands like a bruise.

She walks toward the door, pausing only briefly.

"For what it's worth," she adds, without turning around, "he didn't love me either."

And then she leaves.

The door clicks shut.

I stare at my reflection, replaying everything that's happened.

James is waiting in the hallway when I step out.

"Are you ready to go?"

I nod. He takes my hand, and we start walking toward the exit. The hallway is quiet. Empty.

"James?" I whisper.

He stops immediately, brows furrowing. "Is everything okay?"

"Yes. I just have a question."

"What is it?"

"Why did you ask me to teach you how to love?"

He tilts his head slightly. "I told you. So I could get a wife."

A small, fragile hope blooms in my chest.

"Why do you want a wife?"

He answers without hesitation.

"A wife is practical. I'm at the age where potential partners will see me as noncommittal or untrustworthy without a family. Marriage corrects that."

The hope flickers.

"Getting a wife is the first step to having a family. Producing an heir to inherit my business when I eventually pass."

Oh.

I swallow.

"Why did you ask me?" I force out.

There's no pause. No reconsideration.

"Because you were the most practical and convenient choice."

Practical.

Convenient.

The words don't echo this time.

They settle.

And for the first time since Thanksgiving… since the porch… I understand exactly what this has always been to him.

An arrangement.

And I was foolish enough to mistake it for something more.

Twenty-Two

JAMES

2006

Something is wrong.

Daisy has been... different these past three weeks.

She's back to being how she was when she first started working at the company.

Polite.

Professional.

Distant.

She no longer lingers in my office or uses my first name.

We no longer spend time together outside of the professional setting.

For Christmas, I invited her to attend an event with me, but she denied and instead asked for a two-week-long vacation for the holiday season.

Her reason? She wanted to spend time with her siblings.

I granted it.

Marcus and Adrian claim that she hasn't been any different with them and that maybe I did something to earn this new treatment, but I denied that possibility.

I tried racking my brain, looking for possible answers, but all that resulted was constant headaches.

That's another problem that has arisen these past three weeks.

My body is behaving inefficiently.

The Symptoms

I wake at 3:17 a.m. most nights.

No identifiable trigger.

My chest feels tight. Not sharp pain, just pressure. Like something sitting directly beneath my sternum.

Appetite reduced by approximately forty percent.

Coffee intake increased.

Focus diminished.

Camera three remains on.

She works without humming now.

I tell myself nothing has changed operationally.

This is temporary.

Variables fluctuate.

They stabilize.

Except she does not.

Attempted Solutions

I test theories.

1 Increased workload?
→ Reduce her assignments.
2 Fatigue?
→ Enforce earlier departures.
3 Interpersonal conflict?
→ Replay our conversation repeatedly.

It took a while before I settled into the brunch conversation. When everything shifted.

"Because you were the most practical and convenient choice."

There was a pause after I said it.

Daisy's face had changed.

I don't understand why.

I answered honestly.

Honesty is optimal.

Yet the system destabilized after that statement.

Correlation noted.

Causation unclear.

The Breaking Point

In the fourth week without adequate sleep, the chest pressure intensifies.

I calculate possibilities:

- *Cardiac event.*
- *Stress-induced hypertension.*
- *Sleep deprivation cascade.*

I scheduled a private appointment.

The office smells sterile, and the lights are too bright. I had countless tests done by the cardiologist.

EKG.

Blood Panel.

Blood Pressure.

Respiratory evaluations.

She studies the results intensely, "Mr. Wyatt, everything looks normal."

"That is incorrect," I reply. "There is persistent thoracic pressure and appetite disruption."

She folds her hands.

"Have there been any recent life changes?"

"No."

A pause.

"Yes."

She waits.

"An interpersonal dynamic shifted."

Her eyebrows rise slightly.

"And how has that affected you?"

"I am not certain. My sleep cycle has been compromised."

She nods slowly.

"This doesn't appear cardiac. It sounds like stress."

"I do not experience stress."

She gives me a look I dislike. It reminds me of the looks Marcus and Adrian give me when I don't understand something they deem as simple.

"Sometimes emotional distress presents physically."

"I am not emotionally distressed."

Another look.

She writes something on a notepad and slides it across the desk.

A referral.

"I'd like you to speak with someone."

"I do not require psychiatric intervention."

"It's not intervention," she says gently. "It's just an assessment."

"Why?"

"Mr. Wyatt, I've been working with you for years," she sighs. "Although it's not my field, I have noticed you are a bit different when it comes to processing and identifying your emotions."

I nod.

"Just," she continues. "Try it out, if it doesn't work. I'll run more tests."

At first, I was tempted to cancel the therapy appointment.

I found it to be useless.

But Marcus and Adrian admitted to knowing something about my condition and how to fix what happened between Daisy and me, but they refused to help.

"You need to learn how to label and differentiate your emotions," Adrian said with an exhausted sigh when I went to him for advice. "We won't always be there to help you."

Marcus was meaner, "Desiree is a nice girl, I'm not going to help you with shit until you grow up."

So I'm in this warm office that has multiple bookshelves and is decorated in neutral tones and soft lighting.

A woman in her late forties, Dr. Lang, extends her hand.

I shake it.

We sit.

She begins, "What brings you here, James?"

"Chest pressure. Insomnia. Appetite suppression."

She nods. "And the doctor ruled out medical causes?"

"Yes."

"Any recent emotional events?"

"I do not categorize events emotionally."

A flicker of interest crosses her face.

"That's interesting."

"It is factual."

She studies me carefully.

"Tell me about the interpersonal dynamic that shifted."

I hesitate, feeling a bit foolish for even doing this.

"There is a woman," I begin. "We entered into a mutually beneficial arrangement."

"And?"

"She has altered her behavior following a conversation in which I provided accurate reasoning for my decisions."

"And what was your reasoning?"

"That she was the most practical and convenient choice."

Dr. Lang's pen pauses mid-note.

"And how did she respond?"

"She withdrew."

Silence.

Then:

"And how did that make you feel?"

The question is inefficient.

"I do not know."

"Try."

"I experienced physiological disruption."

"That's not a feeling."

I lean back slightly.

"Then I do not have the appropriate classification."

She nods slowly.

"James, do you struggle with identifying or interpreting emotions? Your own or others'?"

"Yes."

Another pause.

"There's a term for difficulty recognizing and describing emotions," she continues carefully. "It's called alexithymia. Sometimes people who operate highly in logic and control develop a kind of emotional blindness. They experience feelings physically, but don't have language for them."

I say nothing.

She watches me.

"Chest pressure," she says gently. "Sleep disturbance. Appetite loss. Those are also common symptoms of heartbreak."

The word feels misplaced.

"I am not heartbroken."

"Maybe," she replies calmly, "Maybe not."

Silence settles between us. Images of her laugh, her little hums, her hugging and crying on my lap flash in my mind.

For the first time in weeks, the tightness in my chest shifts.

Not gone.

But... *identified?*

Dr. Lang folds her hands.

"Let's start at the beginning," she says. "Tell me about this woman."

And for reasons I cannot logically justify,

I do.

DESIREE

2006

Spring arrives quietly.

In small shifts. Warmer air. Longer evenings. The scent of something new is trying to grow.

I try to do the same.

Move on quietly.

Forget James Wyatt quietly.

It should be easy.

He hasn't crossed a single line, ever.

Hasn't lingered.

Hasn't invited me anywhere after I denied the first time,

Hasn't called me Daisy outside of the rare slip when we're alone, and even then, he corrects himself.

He acts like everything is fine.

Like nothing changed.

Like, I didn't walk away from that hallway conversation feeling like I had just been categorized in a spreadsheet.

Practical.

Convenient.

So I decided to be practical too.

I start dating.

I first went on a date with a finance analyst. He was harmless and funny.

Dinner went well. He laughed at my jokes. Asked about my siblings. Complimented my dress.

He texted me after.

Had a great time. Let's do this again.

Then silence.

No response the next day.

Or the day after that.

Ghosted.

My second date was with a lawyer. He was confident, a bit arrogant, but still attractive.

We had drinks, and he walked me to my apartment. I'm not ashamed to say we had a little fun before he left.

The next morning?

His number was disconnected.

My last date happened on valentines day, it was in the morning, and we were having a coffee.

The date didn't make it past that.

He excused himself to take a call and never came back.

I took that as a sign to stop dating and focus on other aspects of my life.

Work.

The only stable thing, despite my employer.

The Annual Company Anniversary Party is approaching, the biggest event of the year.

This year marks eight years since James took over.

It has to be flawless.

Spring theme.

Light florals. Soft greens. Ivory linens. Hanging installations of wisteria and glass lanterns.

I throw myself into planning.

Vendor contracts. Guest lists. Seating charts. Catering tastings.

James gives input when required, but mostly leaves me to it.

He trusts me.

Professionally.

Always professionally.

"You've outdone yourself," Adrian says one afternoon while reviewing the finalized layout.

"Thank you," I reply.

Marcus studies me for a second longer than necessary.

"You look thinner," he comments casually. "Have you been skipping meals?"

"I'm not."

He hums like he doesn't believe me.

"Why are you guys here anyway?" I ask. "Aren't you guys usually with Mr. Wyatt?"

They both glance at each other, a silent conversation between them, before Adrian responds.

"He's at his weekly appointment," He says like it's nothing.

"Plus, why can't we hang out with you?" Marcus teases. "Aren't we all friends?"

I go back to my work, not entertaining them. My mind going to what Adrian said.

Only one thing has changed with James, every week he has these private meetings that I don't know much about. He just randomly asked me to block off the time and left it at that.

I find myself wondering what it could be, and I'm sure if I ask him, he would tell me, but I don't bother.

Because asking would mean caring.

And caring doesn't help with moving on.

The night of the party arrives.

The venue looks exactly how I envisioned it.

Soft blush lighting. Fresh florals everywhere. A string quartet near the entrance transitions into a live band deeper inside the hall.

Employees mingle. Investors circulate. Laughter fills the room.

I wear a pale green dress that Crystal insisted makes my body "look illegal."

I ignore that comment.

James arrives an hour into the event.

Black suit. No tie. Crisp white shirt.

Effortlessly composed.

He pauses when he steps inside.

His eyes scan the room.

Then they land on me, and stay.

Something in my stomach tightened as he approached slowly.

"Ms. Johnson," he says formally.

"Mr. Wyatt."

A flicker passes through his expression. Gone before I can analyze it.

"The decor is... impressive."

"Thank you."

Silence stretches between us.

People move around us, laughing, drinking, unaware of the tension sitting quietly in the space we're not closing.

"You've done exceptional work," he adds.

"I always do."

It comes out sharper than intended.

His jaw tightens slightly, "I didn't mean—"

"I know what you meant," I cut in gently. "It's fine."

It's fine.

Those two words feel like the biggest lie I've ever told.

Marcus appears suddenly at my side.

"James, can I steal you for a second?" he asks too casually.

Adrian joins me on my other side. "Actually, both of you. There's an office upstairs we can use."

"I'm hosting," I protest lightly.

"It'll take two minutes," Adrian assures.

It does not take two minutes.

The second we step into the office, the door shuts behind us.

And locks.

There's an audible click.

I turn.

"Marcus?"

Silence.

Footsteps retreating.

Adrian's muffled voice through the door, "Communicate like adults!"

I stare at the handle.

"You have got to be kidding me."

James walks toward the door and tests it once.

Locked.

He exhales slowly through his nose.

"This is highly unprofessional."

"Your friends don't seem to care."

"They rarely do."

Silence again.

The office suddenly feels smaller than usual. The music from the party is distant now.

Just bass through walls.

I cross my arms. "They'll open it eventually."

"Yes."

Neither of us moves.

I avoid looking at him.

He does not avoid looking at me.

"Dai—" he stops himself. "Desiree."

The name lands differently.

"What?" I ask.

His hands flex slightly at his sides. A tell I've learned means he's thinking too hard.

"You've been... different."

I let out a humorless laugh, "Have I?"

"Yes."

"Interesting."

His expression shifts, not anger. Not confusion.

Something heavier.

"I am attempting," he says carefully, "to understand what changed."

I finally look at him fully.

"You don't know?"

"If I did, I would have corrected it."

Corrected it.

Like it's a code error.

"That's the problem," I whisper.

His brow furrows. "Explain."

"You don't fix people, James. You don't optimize emotions. You don't categorize relationships into cost-benefit analyses."

"I was honest."

"You were clinical."

Silence.

"I asked why you chose me," I continue. "And you said I was convenient."

"That was accurate."

My throat tightens.

"Do you hear yourself?"

He goes still.

For once, he doesn't respond immediately.

"I believed," he says slowly, "that honesty was preferable to fabrication."

"It is," I nod. "But so is consideration."

His jaw shifts slightly. Processing.

I shake my head. "It doesn't matter. This was always temporary."

"That was the initial agreement."

"Yes."

"And yet," he adds quietly, "you appear affected by its conclusion."

The words hit like ice water.

"So you admit it's over."

"I did not say that."

"You didn't have to."

The room feels too warm.

I look toward the door again.

"I started dating," I say before I can stop myself.

Something changes instantly.

Not subtle, like usual.

His posture straightens. His shoulders go rigid.

JAMES

2006

"I started dating."

I knew.

Of course, I knew.

The first one was harmless. Finance analyst. Clean record. Mild gambling issue in college, but nothing significant. Dinner lasted two hours and seventeen minutes.

The second one, lawyer. Arrogant. Slightly predatory tone in prior complaints filed against him that never went public.

The third, the Valentine's date, was the most irritating. He excused himself mid-coffee and never returned.

I did not interfere.

I did not make a single call.

But I have an idea who might've and why.

I don't tell Daisy that.

Because right now, none of that matters.

What matters is that she is standing in front of me.

And she is admitting to me that she's dating.

My spine locks.

There is a violent tightening in my chest, sharper than before. Not dull pressure. Not insomnia discomfort.

Something territorial.

Something ugly.

"You're dating," I repeat.

"Yes."

"With intention?"

She blinks. "What does that even mean?"

"Are you seeking permanence?"

Her stare turns incredulous. "Oh, my God."

I should stop speaking.

Dr. Lang said when overwhelmed, pause.

I do not pause, "You did not inform me."

Her eyebrows shoot up. "I don't report to you outside of work."

"That is not what I meant."

"Then what did you mean?"

I don't know.

The words stack behind my teeth with no proper order.

"I was under the impression," I begin carefully, "that your withdrawal was... temporary."

"It was self-preservation."

I go still.

"That hallway conversation," she continues, voice tight, "you made it clear what I was."

"I did not define you."

"You categorized me."

"That was not my intention."

"Intent doesn't erase impact."

I inhale sharply.

Remembering what I have been learning from Dr. Lang.

Use language.

Name the feeling.

"I find your dating... destabilizing."

She laughs once. "Destabilizing."

"Yes."

"Why?"

Because I cannot breathe when I think about it.

Because every time you walked into the office after one of those dates, I had to assess the man's background to determine if he deserved proximity to you.

Because I have been unraveling for three months.

Instead, I say, "It introduces variables."

She stares at me like I'm speaking a different language.

"You are unbelievable."

"I am attempting to be transparent."

"No, you're attempting to be logical."

Silence stretches.

Something in me snaps. The words left me before I could approve, "I am in therapy."

Her expression shifts instantly. Confusion. Surprise.

"What?"

"I am attending weekly sessions."

"Why?"

The answer comes out wrong. Too fast.

"Because I cannot sleep."

She freezes.

"I wake at 3:17 a.m. consistently. My appetite has decreased significantly. I experience thoracic pressure and intermittent shortness of breath."

Her voice softens. "James..."

"I believed it was cardiac."

"Is it?"

"No."

"Then what is it?"

I drag a hand through my hair, something I never do.

"Heartbreak," I say flatly.

The word feels foreign in my mouth.

She goes completely still.

"What?"

"I was informed the symptoms align with heartbreak."

Silence.

The music downstairs pulses faintly through the floor.

"I am frustrated," I continue, the words spilling without structure now. "I am on sleep medication that does not work. Anti-anxiety medication that I do not require. Breathing exercises that are ineffective. And none of it resolves the primary disruption."

Her eyes are wide.

"And what's that?" she whispers.

"You."

The room feels too small.

"You withdrew," I continue, voice tightening. "You stopped saying my name. You stopped humming. You stopped lingering. And I cannot function at optimal capacity without accounting for your absence."

Her breath catches.

"I did not understand why the word convenient altered your perception so drastically. It was not an insult. It was logic. You are efficient. Capable. Trusted. You are the only person whose presence reduces rather than increases my stress levels."

I step closer without realizing it.

"God, Daisy," the name slips out raw this time, uncorrected. "I cannot sleep. I cannot eat. I cannot breathe without you in proximity."

The last sentence hangs between us.

Her hand trembles slightly.

"You're heartbroken?" she asks quietly.

"I do not like that classification," I mutter.

"But it fits?"

"Yes."

"Because of me?"

"Yes."

The word feels like an impact.

She stares at me like I've just handed her something fragile.

"You said I was convenient."

"You are."

Her face falls.

"And necessary," I add quickly, frustration bleeding through. "And stabilizing. And the only person who has ever made me voluntarily attend therapy."

Her lips part.

"I did not select you solely because you were practical," I continue, words accelerating now. "I selected you because you were the only person I trusted not to manipulate me. The only person who did not treat me like an acquisition. The only person who made the concept of permanence seem... tolerable."

She steps closer.

"You are not an asset," I say hoarsely. "You are the disruption."

A tear slips down her cheek.

"And I do not want you dating anyone else."

There.

It's out.

She searches my face.

"You don't want me to date," she repeats.

"No."

"Why?"

I swallow.

"Because I am in love with you."

The words land heavily.

I do not flinch. I do not retract.

They are accurate.

For a long second, she does nothing.

Then she reaches up, slow, deliberate, and grabs my suit jacket.

"You are so bad at this," she whispers.

"I am aware."

And then she kisses me.

Her hand fists my collar, and she rises on her toes, pressing her mouth to mine like she is sealing something.

It is not soft. It is desperate and warm and undeniable.

For a fraction of a second, I freeze.

Then I respond.

My hands slide to her waist, pulling her closer, anchoring her against me.

The world narrows.

Nothing else matters

Just her.

When she pulls back, her forehead rests against mine.

"You're still an idiot," she murmurs.

"Statistically probable."

She laughs against my mouth.

Downstairs, the music swells.

We remain there for a moment longer before someone unlocks the door from the outside.

Marcus' voice drifts in. "You two alive?"

"Yes," I answer evenly.

Daisy glares at the door. "You're dead," she mutters.

Later that evening, when Daisy is occupied with vendors near the stage, I find Marcus and Adrian near the bar.

Adrian studies my face once and smirks. "Well."

Marcus raises his glass. "You're welcome."

"For locking us in," I say calmly.

"For forcing you to man up," Adrian corrects.

There is a brief pause.

"And," Marcus adds casually, "for handling those idiots she kept going out with."

I hold his gaze.

"I assumed."

"They weren't good enough," Adrian shrugs. "We did you a favor."

"We did her a favor," Marcus corrects.

I nod once.

"Thank you."

They both blink.

Marcus squints. "Did you just—"

"Yes."

Adrian laughs softly. "Therapy working?"

"Incrementally."

Marcus claps my shoulder. "Told you heartbreak would fix you."

I glance across the room.

Daisy is laughing with a vendor, pale green dress catching the light.

"No," I say quietly.

"She did."

And for the first time in months,

I slept well that night.

Twenty-Five

DESIREE

2027

"I can't believe we're just leaving her there," I sob to James the minute we get in the car. "She looked so small in that building. Did you see how big the hallway was? What if she forgets to eat? What if she—"

"Daisy."

James' voice is steady, low. Grounded.

I turn to him, eyes wet. "She's nineteen."

"Yes."

"She's never lived anywhere without us," I continue through my sob. "I mean, yes, we would leave her home alone at times, and she's pretty independent, but it's not the same."

"Do you want me to go back to monitoring her?" He asks, trying to make me feel better.

I shake my head, "N-no, I want her to have a proper college experience."

He stays silent.

I continue my worried rant, "What if she falls, hurts herself, and we find out too late?"

"We won't," he reassures. "And we now live twenty minutes away. We will see her often."

Finally, I voice the main concern, "W-what if something like what happened before, happens again?"

He starts the car but doesn't pull away yet. His hand rested on the steering wheel longer than necessary.

I watch his jaw clench as he remembers what our daughters' been through. And how he hated himself for not being able to prevent it.

"It won't," He says through clenched teeth. "The campus security is great. And I trust that boyfriend of hers to keep her safe when I'm not around."

I look at him in surprise, "You trust Azrail?"

"He's adequate."

I stifle a laugh.

"And we have raised her to defend herself," he adds. "I trust she will hold her own."

I sniff, wiping my face with the sleeve of my cardigan. "I miss her already."

He reaches over, cupping the back of my neck and pulling me gently toward him. I leaned across the center console without hesitation.

"I know," he murmurs into my hair. "I miss her too."

For a moment, we just sit there like that. Breathing each others scent.

"She didn't even cry," I whisper.

"She did not want you to."

That breaks me all over again.

After a few minutes, I pull back and try to compose myself. "I can't believe we're going to be empty nesters."

"Yes, time flies."

"It's going to be so quiet."

"We will find ways to fill it."

I stare out the windshield. Then, because I cope with sadness by making terrible suggestions, I say lightly.

"Well.. we could always have another one."

Silence.

I don't look at him at first.

Then I do.

He's frozen.

Completely still. Not blinking or breathing. His hands tighten on the steering wheel like he's just been informed of an unexpected danger."

"... James?"

His throat moved once. "Another child."

My eyes widen at his words, reality hitting me. I quickly reach for his hands, squeezing them to comfort him.

"Hey..." I say softly. "I was joking. I didn't mean it, just a joke, just a joke."

He gives a stiff nod and repeats absentmindedly, "Just a joke."

He pulls off the parking lot, one hand on the wheel and the other in mine as I draw comforting circles on his palm.

Twenty-Six

DESIREE

2007

The house smells like pine, cinnamon, and roasting chestnuts. I adjust the wreath on the front door and take a deep breath, smiling at the way the Christmas lights catch on the new windows.

Our first Christmas in this house. James and I.

My eyes water at the thought. I still can't believe everything that's happened in the past year. After the night Marcus and Adrian locked us in that office, James and I have been inseparable.

In the first three months alone, he rebuilt the top floor of the company—expanding his office and connecting mine to it—because he "didn't want to be far from me."

A normal person would probably hate the clinginess.

I adore it.

He lingers without realizing it, disguising his needs as practicality and logistical improvements.

I still remember when he showed me the renovation.

"Having your office closer to mine means you don't have to travel as far," he explained. "Which increases efficiency."

"And?" I teased. "It took a mere ten paces from my old office to yours."

"Now it takes five," he replied smoothly. "Increasing productivity by fifty percent."

"James?" I walked up to him and fixed his tie. "Stop being logical and use your words."

He closed his eyes, inhaled slowly, and gave in. "I don't want to be far from you. I love having you close. But if it's too much, you don't have to."

I kissed him quickly. "I'd love to."

"Daisy, you look radiant," James says now from behind me, his hand sliding around my waist, cradling my barely-there bump.

I glance down at my stomach and laugh softly. "Radiant or round?"

"It suits you," he says, eyes crinkling in that way I've come to love. "You look adorable."

That's another thing that's changed.

I'm three months pregnant with our first child.

Our first of many.

James knew before I did. I didn't even realize he had been tracking my cycle until he came home one day with a pregnancy test and calmly instructed me to take it.

I was over the moon.

James was... well, James.

More possessive. More cautious. More attentive than ever.

The doorbell rings.

"Oh, they're here," I cheer, breaking our embrace to greet our guests.

Another thing that's changed: I've fallen in love with hosting.

Dinner parties, holidays, random Sundays. And James lets me host as many as I want without complaint.

The door swings open to chaos.

Carol and her family arrive first. Joseph runs straight to James and wraps his arms around his legs.

"Hi, Uncle James!"

"Hi, buddy," James replies, bending slightly to return the hug.

The rest of my siblings follow. Then Marcus and Adrian, carrying gifts and alcohol like they own the place.

They're the only ones who know about the pregnancy so far. James needed advice on whether he should tell me or let me figure it out myself.

It was mildly humiliating to discover the men in my life knew before I did, but they've been spoiling me nonstop since, so I suppose I'll survive.

Last to arrive are my parents, Lauren, JJ, and their three children, all under five.

I didn't exactly forgive them. But I chose to leave the past where it belongs. And my nieces and nephews are adorable—it's not their fault they have questionable parents and grandparents.

I first made peace when I invited them to our wedding this summer. My parents were "apologetic." Lauren and JJ learned quickly not to provoke me.

Something tells me that has a lot to do with the private conversation Crystal saw James having with JJ during the reception while I was busy.

I didn't ask.

I simply enjoyed the peace.

The house fills quickly, laughter, children running down the hall, boots by the door, coats tossed over chairs, the clink of wine glasses.

I float through it all, warm and light and slightly hormonal, nursing ginger ale like it's champagne.

James stations himself subtly at my side. A hand at my lower back. Fingers brushing my waist whenever someone gets too close. His eyes track every movement in the room without making it obvious.

"Relax," I murmur under my breath.

"I am relaxed," he replies evenly.

He is not relaxed.

I hide my smile and step forward, lifting my glass.

"Okay, everyone," I say, tapping gently. "Before we eat, I have something to say."

The room quiets gradually. Conversations taper off. All eyes turn to me.

"We're pregnant," I say, my smile brightening as I glance at James. "About three months."

For a moment, everything is silent. And then, cheers. Tears. Laughter. My siblings squeal, my parents' eyes glisten, and the kids bounce around, demanding explanations. Marcus and Adrian celebrate like it's their first time hearing the news.

James turns to me and smiles. His hand slides protectively over my stomach like he can feel the tiny life inside.

"Our first of many," I tease.

"Let us achieve successful completion of one before planning multiples," he mutters.

Laughter ripples around us.

Marcus claps James on the shoulder. "You're going to be terrifying as a father."

"That's the plan," James replies calmly.

More laughter.

Dinner grows louder after that. Stories, congratulations, my mom and sisters sharing birth experiences. Adrian makes a comment about the next generation of "genetic overachievers" being secured.

Later, when the noise splits into smaller conversations, I find James alone in our room.

He's staring at the ultrasound picture like it's a classified file.

"You okay?" I ask softly.

He nods.

Then shakes his head.

"I am... concerned."

"About?"

He exhales slowly.

"My issues," he says plainly. "If the baby inherits my emotional processing deficits. Or worse." His jaw tightens. "And since we both carry the recessive gene.... The statistical probability—"

Right. That gene.

When we first went to the doctor, routine questions about medical history led to unexpected answers. That's how we discovered we both carry the recessive gene for congenital insensitivity to pain—the condition that prevents someone from feeling pain.

It runs in my family. I knew that.

James didn't. With his parents gone and no extended family, he had no idea.

"James."

He stops. His eyes flick to my stomach.

"I do not want them to struggle," he admits. "I do not want them to feel isolated. Or different. Or unsafe in their own body."

The vulnerability in that confession makes my chest ache.

"He won't be alone," I say gently. "And we're not guessing. We can get prenatal testing. We'll know early. We'll prepare."

He studies me like he's recalibrating.

"Testing would reduce uncertainty," he says slowly.

"Yes."

He nods once. "Then we will proceed with testing."

I step forward and take his face in my hands.

"You don't have to solve everything tonight."

"I am aware."

"You're allowed to just be happy."

He looks at me like that concept still feels foreign.

"I am happy," he says quietly. "I am also afraid."

"That's normal."

"For me?"

"For anyone."

He rests his forehead against mine.

"I will not allow harm to come to you," he murmurs.

"I know."

I laugh softly and kiss him.

Out in the living room, someone calls my name. Glasses clink. Christmas music hums faintly in the background.

I press his hand back over my stomach.

"We're going to be okay," I whisper.

He inhales, steadying.

"Yes," he says finally. "We are."

And for the first time since I told him, his shoulders lowered just slightly.

"I love you, Mr.Wyatt."

He pulls me in for a brief kiss.

"I love you more, Mrs.Wyatt."

Twenty-Seven

JAMES

2008

Today we find out our baby's gender. I wanted to wait a big longer so we could be certain, but Daisy insisted on going as soon as possible for the good news.

We're currently in the office waiting for the technician to do the ultrasound. Daisy was bouncing off the wall.

"Ah, can you believe it James," She squeals with excitement, rubbing her bump. It's starting to be a bit more obvious now. "We find out our baby's gender today."

"We might not," I comment, not wanting to have high hopes and be disappointed. "They could have their legs crossed and-"

"James," she cuts me off with a glare that I'm sure is meant to be intimidating. "No negativity."

"I'm not trying to be negative, my love, just being logical."

She lets out an exhausted sigh, "Well, either be optimistic or take that logic outside."

I flinch at her tone, "Sorry."

Her frown turns upside-down immediately. She hops out of

bed and gives me a big kiss. I pull her down on my lap, deepening it, loving how her body feels against mine.

I've never been one to fall for carnal pleasures, never felt the need for it. But Daisy, she awakened a lot of firsts, and I can't get enough.

"Ahem."

The technician interrupts us. Daisy is quick to get off of me, mumbling an apology before getting on the bed with my help

"You two are the cutest," She comments. "Reminds me when I first got married, we couldn't keep our hands off of each other."

"Did it ever stop?" Daisy asks, squeezing my hand.

That earns a small chuckle from the technician, a blush forming on her cheeks, "Never, I have to beat him off with a stick just to come to work."

I imagine Daisy and me ten, twenty, thirty years from now. Our kids out of the house, lazy afternoons, endless kisses, and love between us.

She squeezed my hands when the ultrasound gel was administered, "Are you okay?"

"Just cold," She mutters, her brow furrowing a bit.

Although she's the optimist between us two, I could see the worry on her face every doctor visit. I know she is bracing herself for some terrible last-minute news.

And honestly... So am I.

"Alright, mom and dad," The technician comments, evaporating our anxiety. "The doctor will be here to tell you the results shortly."

"Can we know the gender?" I ask before Daisy can stop me.

The technician smiles knowingly. "Impatient, aren't we?"

Daisy squeezes my hand. "He pretends he isn't."

The door opens, and the doctor steps in, chart in hand. He greets us, reviews a few measurements first—heartbeat steady, growth on track, development appropriate for gestational age. I catalog each word carefully, committing it to memory.

Daisy exhales slowly beside me. I didn't realize she'd been holding her breath.

"And as for the gender..." The doctor tilts his head, angling the image.

There's a pause.

Then a smile.

"Congratulations."

He turns the screen slightly toward us.

"It's a girl."

For a moment, the room goes silent.

A girl.

Daisy gasps, a bright, overwhelmed sound, before covering her mouth. Tears immediately fill her eyes.

"A girl?" she repeats.

"A very stubborn one," the technician laughs lightly. "She's moving quite a bit."

I feel something crack open in my chest.

A daughter.

My daughter.

Daisy turns to me, eyes shining. "James."

I don't trust my voice. I lean down and press my forehead to hers instead.

A girl.

The technician prints out photos for us. Daisy clutches them like they're fragile relics.

I take Daisy to lunch afterward.

We end up at a quiet restaurant overlooking the river. Daisy insists on sitting near the window. She keeps pulling the ultrasound photos from her purse to stare at them again, as though they might disappear if she doesn't check.

"A girl," she whispers, almost to herself. "James, we're having a daughter."

"I am aware," I reply, though my voice lacks its usual dryness.

She studies me carefully. "You're quiet."

"I am calculating."

She narrows her eyes playfully. "Calculating what?"

"Security systems. Educational planning. Long-term investment portfolios. Potential threats."

She laughs. "James."

"I will need to reevaluate several aspects of our lives."

"For a baby?"

"For a daughter."

Her smile softens.

"She's going to love you," Daisy says gently.

I look down at the ultrasound photo in my hand. The small curve that will become her nose. The outline of her skull.

"She will be protected," I say quietly.

Daisy reaches across the table and squeezes my hand.

Throughout lunch, Daisy talks the entire time. Talks of name, dresses, tiny shoes, and how she always wanted a daughter.

I listen.

I imagine a small hand wrapped around my finger.

I imagine her first steps.

Her first word.

Her first day of school.

"She's going to wrap you around her finger," Daisy teases, stirring her soup.

"That is statistically unlikely."

Daisy raises a brow.

I exhale. "It is highly probable."

She laughs, radiant.

"Have you thought about the nursery?" she asks.

"Yes."

She blinks. "You have?"

"Extensively."

Her smile widens. "Tell me."

"I will repaint it," I begin. "The current shade is too neutral. We will need something softer. Perhaps ivory with pale green accents. Reinforced shelving. Rounded furniture edges. Secured fixtures. I've already contacted someone about installing additional temperature regulation and improved air filtration."

"James," she says gently, amused. "It's a baby room, not a laboratory."

"It will be both."

She reaches across the table and takes my hand. "You're going to be an amazing father."

I look down at our joined hands, "I will try."

After lunch, we stop at the home store. I buy the paint samples while Daisy browses for inspiration.

That night, after Daisy falls asleep, I stand inside the empty room and imagine it filled.

A crib near the window.

A bookshelf.

A rocking chair.

Her name is written on the wall.

Aisha.

I say it quietly in the dark.

Aisha Wyatt.

And for the first time in my life, I feel something dangerously close to peace

Twenty-Eight

JAMES

2008

The phone call comes on a Tuesday afternoon.

Daisy answers it on speaker while I stand beside her in the kitchen. She smiles at first, expecting confirmation of normal results.

Her smile fades before the doctor even finishes the sentence.

"I'm sorry," the doctor says gently. "The genetic testing indicates your daughter has inherited the mutation."

Silence.

I feel Daisy's fingers searching blindly for mine.

"The condition presents differently in every case," the doctor continues. "But congenital insensitivity to pain can significantly impact life expectancy if not managed carefully. Historically, complications can reduce lifespan."

Reduce lifespan.

Daisy swallows. "How reduced?"

"There is no exact number," the doctor replies. "But statistically..."

I stop listening.

The room becomes very quiet.

Low lifespan.

My daughter.

The call eventually ends. I don't remember how.

Daisy is crying softly beside me.

"We'll manage it," she says quickly. "We'll be careful. We'll baby-proof everything. We'll teach her—"

"Yes," I interrupt.

My voice sounds distant.

Controlled.

Precise.

I begin outlining modifications out loud.

Environmental safeguards. Medical specialists. Home adjustments. Continuous monitoring protocols.

Daisy watches me.

"James."

"We will reduce risk variables."

"James."

"I will not allow preventable injury."

She steps in front of me, forcing me to look at her.

"Are you with me?"

"I am here."

But something inside me is already retreating.

I do not sleep that night.

Or the next.

I spend hours researching case studies. Mortality rates. Adaptive strategies.

I begin detaching the way I do when loss becomes statistically probable.

It is easier to prepare for grief than to feel hope.

2008

The day was as ordinary as it could've been.

With Daisy's due date approaching soon, we both took leave from work.

Daisy permanently, me for three months.

Daisy spent the majority of the day in bed, too tired to walk around. I brought her food, and we watched as many romcoms as she wanted.

It was midway through *27 Dresses* when Daisy hunched over in pain. Tears pricked her eyes as she looked over to me to tell me her water broke.

It was 2:17 AM.

The drive to the hospital was swift. We were staying at my penthouse near the hospital this week for moments like this. Yet, Daisy's contractions intensified faster than anticipated.

By the time we arrived, Daisy's knuckles were white from gripping my hand, and we could see a bit of blood.

The nurse moves us to the room quickly. Attaching my wife to machines and wires.

My daughter's heart rate is said to be irregular.

My wife's blood pressure dropping rapidly.

Multiple voices overlapping.

"Prepare for an emergency C-section."

They begin wheeling her away from me. Daisy's fingers tighten around mine, "James."

Her voice is weak. Scared.

I lean down, pressing my forehead to hers. "I'm here."

"I-If something happens—" she starts to cry.

"Nothing will happen," I interrupt sharply.

It was the first time I found myself lying to my wife. The first time, I'm not certain of an outcome.

The first time I knew that my money, my influence, and my connection wouldn't be able to help me.

Despite my protests, I'm not allowed to be in the operating room. The nurses and doctors pushed me into the waiting area with nothing but fluorescent lights and the echo of Daisy's strained breathing in my head.

A doctor approaches me ten minutes later. Or maybe it was thirty. Time fractures.

"There are complications," he says carefully. "We're doing everything we can."

"For both?" I ask.

He hesitates.

"If it comes to it," he continues, "we may need you to make a decision.

My heart stops.

"Between my wife and my daughter," I say flatly.

He doesn't answer. He doesn't need to.

The world narrows into a single unbearable point.

My thoughts turn violent.

If I pick Aisha, Daisy dies, and Aisha is left without knowing her mother. She will have to live with the fact that I played a hand in her mother's death.

If I pick Daisy, Aisha dies, and Daisy is left without her daughter. She will have to live with the fact that I killed our daughter.

If I don't pick, both—

My chest constricts so tightly I cannot breathe.

For the first time in my life, I understand the appeal of oblivion.

If they are gone, there is no version of reality in which I continue.

I stand abruptly, pacing.

A voice interrupts me.

"Mr. Wyatt, what are you doing here?"

I pause. Turning to the voice, my eyes landed on Officer Walker.

"Howard," My voice, unrecognizable by me. "What are you doing here?"

"Jack had a fever," He answers, referring to his two-year-old son. "I left to get some food for his mom. She's been so stressed that she hasn't eaten yet."

"Is he better?" I attempt at small talk.

Anything to keep my mind off of what's happening in the operating room.

"Yes," He answers with a fond smile. "They're just keeping him the night for observation."

I nod, "That's good."

We stand in silence for a beat before Howard clears his throat, "So um," He shifts. "What brings you here?"

"My wife," I manage. "Emergency surgery."

He nods slowly, a sympathetic look on his face. I don't need to say much for him to understand. He's seen Daisy waddling around with her pregnant belly.

Daisy.

I feel my knees buckle beneath me, the reality of it all too much to bear. I'm not sure how long I stay seated there, not even sure when the tears start to fall.

"If I lose them," My voice raw and unrecognizable. "If I lose any of them due to my decision. I- I don't know what I'll do. I might..."

I don't let the words leave my lips, I don't need to. Howard knew exactly what I meant.

"They're stronger than we think," Howard says, attempting to reassure me. "You've got to stay steady, they need you."

A cry pierces the hallway. Sharp. Strong. Defiant.

A nurse rushes out, smiling at me. "Congratulations, Mr. Wyatt. A beautiful babygirl."

I feel blood pulsing in my ear, "And my wife?" I choke.

"Stable. She lost a lot of blood, but she's stable," She says with a big smile. "The doctor is closing her up."

The world rushes back in all at once. For the first time since I've been in this hospital, I allow myself relax.

They're both okay.

Time passes fast before another nurse comes to get me. I follow her into a private room.

Daisy is pale against the white sheets, attached to tubes and machines. She's sleeping, so I don't bother her. I look by her side, and that's when I meet her. The tiniest human being I've ever seen.

Aisha.

She lies in a small bassinet. Like a perfect tiny angel.

I step closer slowly, placing one careful gloved finger in her palm.

She grips it immediately.

I look over to Daisy, whose eyes are now open, and she gives me a weak smile.

"You're okay," I breathe.

She nods. I look back at Aisha, who was wiggling around the bassinet, still gripping my finger.

"She's so small," I comment.

Daisy clears her throat, "W-who does she look like?" Her voice was dry and tiny.

"You," I answer without a second thought. "Exactly like you."

Daisy smiles fondly before looking at me, her eyes watering in tears, "J-james?"

I quickly leave Aisha's side, going by her side and holding he arms, "Yes, Daisy."

"I-I don't e-ever w-want to do that again?" She sobs.

I pull her into a hug, "And you won't ever have to. I promise."

And in that instant, as Daisy cries in my arms and Aisha coos in the bassinet, I understand something with terrifying clarity.

I will burn the world down before I lose either of them.

Even if it destroys me.

Twenty-Nine

DESIREE

2008

The house is louder than it has ever been, and for good reason, too.

Last year I hosted a party to announce my pregnancy; this year I'm hosting another to celebrate.

Aisha turned six months old last week.

Six whole months.

The pediatric specialist said if Aisha made it past this mark, the risk of sudden infant death related to her condition would drop significantly. Not gone, but lower.

And that's enough to throw a party.

Nothing too large. Just my siblings, Marcys, Adrian, and a few close friends.

But still... a party.

A celebration for surviving.

I look around the living room. Decorations everywhere. Balloons shaped like stars. A cake in the center that reads *Half a Year of Aisha.*

Joseph and the other kids are running down the hallway while my sister argues over what a baby's first hard food should be.

The whole house smells like food and sweets.

And in the middle of it all is, surprisingly, James.

He's standing near the couch, holding Aisha like she's the most delicate object in the world.

Which, to him, she is.

He barely lets anyone else hold her. When he does, he stands within arm's reach, watching like a hawk.

Marcus once joked that James had memorized every breathing pattern Aisha had ever made.

I don't think it was a joke.

Aisha squeals in his arms, grabbing his tie with surprising strength.

"She's strong," Adrian says, sipping his drink. "That's a good sign."

James nods once. "Grip strength is above average for her age."

"James," I say dryly. "She's a baby, not a lab result."

He glances at me, then back at Aisha, who is currently trying to eat his tie.

I walk over and take her carefully.

James hesitates before letting go.

The hesitation tells me everything.

He has been like this ever since we came home from the hospital.

Unlike the stories I was told by my mother and sister, James took care of everything regarding Aisha.

He didn't even hire help.

He didn't trust anyone but him to look over him.

"You can relax," I say.

"I am relaxed."

"You installed three new cameras in the nursery this morning."

"That was preventative," he replies calmly. "We have a lot of guests today. If she wakes up from her nap, we might not hear her."

"James."

He doesn't respond.

Aisha grabs my hair, smiling at me, and I laugh.

Then Walker says something that makes the laughter die in my throat.

"I knew everything would work out," he says casually to James. "Imagine if you had committed suicide that day. You wouldn't have the chance to see your beautiful family today."

Everything goes silent.

I snap my head toward James.

He freezes.

Adrian and Marcus, who are standing nearby, also freeze—then glare at Walker.

And by the look on their faces, I know this was meant to be a secret.

Clearly, Walker forgot.

I turn slowly toward my husband.

"James."

He doesn't answer.

"James," I repeat, quieter this time.

Everyone in the room suddenly finds something else to do.

I hand Aisha to Carol without looking away from him.

"Bedroom. Now."

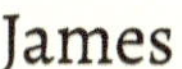

James

Daisy is angry.

This is obvious.

Her footsteps are sharp as she walks upstairs.

I follow.

Behind us, Howard mutters something that sounds suspiciously like *my bad.*

The bedroom door shuts.

Then locks.

Daisy turns around slowly.

"What," she asks, very calmly, "did Howard mean?"

I consider my options.

"He was just making commentary."

"That's not what I asked."

Her eyes are bright with something dangerous.

"James."

Silence.

I finally answer, "I was evaluating outcomes."

Her stare goes blank.

"Evaluating outcomes," she repeats.

"Yes."

Her breathing changes.

It's sharp. Filled with panic.

"You were going to end your life."

"I didn't say that, per se."

"You didn't have to," she snaps.

I try to explain.

"I couldn't live with myself if either of you died due to my decis-"

"Stop," Her voice cracks like a whip. "Stop talking."

I stop.

Daisy presses her hands to her face.

"You idiot," she whispers.

I do not respond.

"You absolute idiot."

She drops her hands and points at me.

"You thought dying was an option?"

"It was a logical contingency."

She actually laughs.

A sharp, angry sound.

"A contingency."

"Yes."

"Six months ago, you were ready to leave me alone with a newborn," she says, voice in disbelief.

Her expression falters for a fraction of a second.

But then the anger comes back stronger.

"So the solution was to abandon your daughter?"

"I would not abandon her."

"You said you wouldn't exist!"

"That was dependent on variables."

Daisy stares at me as if I have personally offended the universe.

"James Wyatt," she says slowly, "if you ever even think about dying before me again, I will resurrect you just to kill you myself."

I consider that statement carefully.

"That seems inefficient."

She throws a pillow at my head

Daisy

I am furious, and James looks genuinely confused.

Which somehow makes it worse.

"You don't get to die," I say.

"I am aware that mortality is generally unavoidable."

I rub my temples, "You don't get to *choose* it."

"I was not choosing it," he insists. "I was acknowledging a possible outcome."

"You were planning it."

"Planning is a strong word."

"James."

"Yes."

"If you died, what would happen to Aisha?"

His mouth opens.

Then closes.

Exactly.

I step closer.

"She needs you."

He doesn't respond.

"And I need you," I add quietly.

The tension in his shoulders shifts slightly.

"You are not allowed to disappear when things get hard," I say.

"I was not disappearing."

"You were giving up."

Silence.

Finally, he says, "I did not know how to survive losing either of you."

My anger softens.

Just a little.

"You wouldn't have to," I say, "because we didn't die."

"Yes."

"So stop preparing for our funerals."

He exhales slowly.

"I will attempt to recalibrate."

"That means stop acting like a paranoid lunatic."

"I am protecting my family."

"You installed biometric locks on the nursery."

"Security is important."

"She's six months old."

"She is vulnerable."

"She is teething."

Apparently, both things are equally serious to my husband.

James

Later that evening, when the party settles down, I sit with Marcus and Adrian on the patio.

Daisy is inside feeding Aisha.

Marcus hands me a drink.

"I've never seen Daisy get this mad at you," he says.

I grumble. The conversation is still replaying in my mind.

Adrian leans back in his chair.

"Well," he says, "on the bright side, I have some updates."

Marcus nods. "We know you stepped away from the business after you and Daisy got together, but we also know you hate being left in the dark."

"That is true."

After marrying Daisy, I stepped away from most operations. Marcus and Adrian handle the business now.

Occasionally, they ask for advice.

Or give me updates.

Like tonight.

"The issues with the Russians and the Japanese are under control," Adrian explains. "You did most of the groundwork anyway."

"And," Marcus adds, "Adrian also decided to help the Whitlocks adopt a child."

"Is that so?"

"Just a few connections in Japan," Adrian says dismissively. "It's a maybe, not a definite."

"Let us hope it doesn't happen," I reply.

I cannot imagine the Whitlocks raising a child.

No matter how desperate they are to have one.

"That being said," Adrian continues, "I'll be making Japan my permanent residence."

That isn't surprising.

He spends most of his time there already.

"You will be missed, my friend," Marcus says dramatically, raising his beer for a toast.

I roll my eyes at his theatrics.

"We will visit often."

"And I the same."

We settle into the silence.

Through the window, I see Daisy in the living room.

Aisha in her arms.

She's laughing at something my sister-in-law says.

My chest settles in a way it rarely does.

Marcus follows my gaze, "Six months," he says.

"Yes."

Adrian raises his glass.

"To the toughest baby alive."

I raise mine.

"To Aisha."

Inside the house, my daughter laughs.

And for tonight, that is enough.

Thirty

JAMES

2027

The campus is quieter than I expected for a Friday afternoon. Leaves crunch beneath my shoes, and the autumn air smells faintly of smoke and damp earth. I enter the building and make my way to my destination.

Room 560.

Azrail's dorm.

I knock once.

"Who is it?" a voice calls.

"James Wyatt," I answer.

The door opens almost instantly. Azrail stands in front of it, a bit more disheveled than usual, his hair sticking out in all directions, his sweats rumpled from a long day.

"M-Mr. Wyatt," he stammers. "Wha-what are you doing here?"

I step in without a word. I don't want anyone to overhear this conversation.

"Close the door," I command.

He does. Immediately.

I glance around the room. The contrast between his side and his roommate's is striking. His space is neat, clean, organized; his roommate's is chaos incarnate.

I lower myself into the chair across from him, careful not to seem too imposing.

"How's school?" I ask, though the question is rhetorical. I've been tracking his grades. Meticulous. Hardworking.

"Good. Busy. Dorm life," he says.

I nod slowly.

"And your roommate isn't giving you any trouble?"

I already know the answer. Just as I do with Aisha's roommates, I've done the same background checks for him. If my daughter is going to love this boy, the least I can do is make sure he's safe.

"N-no, sir."

I let the silence linger a moment.

"Azrail... I need to give you something."

From my pocket, I pull a card. Adrian's.

"If you ever want to know the truth about your adoption, or your biological parents, this is your way to reach him. No pressure. No obligation. Just... the option."

Azrail stares at the card like it's alien.

"Why... why are you giving this to me?"

"He will have all the answers you need," I say calmly, sidestepping the question.

"B-but how?"

"My daughter is the most precious thing in the world to me," I answer. "I might not have been emotionally present in the way she wanted, but I make sure she's always safe. I know everything. No secret gets past me."

I emphasize the last words. I watch his eyes widen.

"There's a world out there you don't know. A dangerous world," I continue. "To know your identity is to know about it. I would rather you not bring my daughter into it, but with your skills, I trust you can protect her."

He swallows a lump in his throat. Silence.

"Why?" he asks again. "Why give me this if you know it's dangerous? If it could bring danger to Aisha?"

"Because you deserve the choice," I say, steady, though tension coils in my chest. "You are strong, smart, capable."

His expression shifts to shock.

"You've given your life to protect my daughter. You've taken life to protect her," I continue. "I believe you deserve the full picture. Adrian can provide it. And you're free to ignore it. Your call."

He studies the card, turning it over in his hands. His jaw tightens. For a moment, I wonder if I've destabilized his world.

"Thanks," he says quietly.

"No rush," I reply. "When you're ready... if you're ready... the choice is yours."

A beat of silence. Then he smirks slightly.

"I'll think about it."

"That's all I ask."

I rise, giving him a small approving nod before heading to the door.

"Mr. Wyatt?" His voice stops me.

"How come you're okay with the deaths?"

I pause, turning slowly.

"I see a bit of myself in you. I'm not perfect," I say. "And I don't pretend to be. I will always protect my family, at the expense of anyone who threatens it."

"They weren't on purpose," he tries to defend. "Just accidents."

I allow a small, controlled laugh. I know he believes that. But my research tells me differently.

"I don't care what you do, Azrail," I say, my tone calm but sharp. "As long as Aisha is safe. As long as she still loves you."

I pause. The weight hangs in the air.

"Then you won't have to worry about me."

He nods slowly.

"I would lay my life down for her, sir."

A genuine smile touches my lips.

"Glad we've come to an agreement."

I stop mid-step, glancing at the pictures of Aisha on his wall.

"Oh, and Asahi... if you insist on drawing her, keep the pictures away from prying eyes. I don't need your roommate or friends staring at my daughter."

"Y-yes, sir."

"And bring a copy during dinner. I want one in my office."

"Yes, sir."

Epilogue

AZRAIL

2027

The dining room smells faintly of roasted chicken and rosemary. Mr. Wyatt sits at the head of the table, Mrs. Wyatt beside him, Aisha across from us, and my mother next to Mrs. Wyatt, facing me.

A pulse of tension hums under the warmth of the room. Family dinners at the Wyatts' are routine, but Mrs. Wyatt and Aisha always insist my mom and I attend. "Your son took a bullet for my daughter. You're basically family now," Mrs. Wyatt had told my mom when she tried to decline. "I won't take no for an answer."

"Pass the salad, Azrail," Mrs. Wyatt says, smiling. I hand it across. "Here you go."

Aisha reaches over and squeezes my hand. I return the gesture quietly, reassuringly. I'm not usually this nervous at family dinners, but since Mr. Wyatt's visit, I've felt a subtle tension around him.

I still haven't contacted Adrian. The thought sits heavy in my chest—not fear, but the weight of responsibility. Everything Mr. Wyatt said last week echoes in quiet insistence.

The conversation drifts around the table. Mrs. Wyatt chats effortlessly with my mother about Aisha's latest performance, her laugh bright and unrestrained. Mr. Wyatt mostly listens, eyes scanning the room, occasionally settling on me. Not in judgment, but in assessment. That same steady, calculated pulse I've felt since he handed me Adrian's card. A reminder of trust earned, responsibility granted.

Aisha squeezes my hand again. She doesn't know about her father's visit, but she senses the thoughts in my mind and reassures me. She's laughing at something her mom said, a high, giddy sound that reminds me of why I love her. Outside, the world is unpredictable, chaotic, dangerous—but here, at this table, it's warm. Safe.

For a moment, the anxiety in my chest loosens.

I join the small talk, pass dishes, nod at jokes. Mr. Wyatt glances my way now and then—sharp, direct, reading me—but it no longer feels intimidating. Since our talk, I realize he's no longer testing me. He's gauging how I carry myself within his family, how I protect what matters.

Finally, the plates are cleared. Mrs. Wyatt whispers something to Aisha, and Mr. Wyatt leans back slightly, eyes softening as he watches them. I excuse myself, muttering about grabbing my coat, though I've been waiting for this moment.

In the quiet of the foyer, I pull out my phone. My thumb hovers over Adrian's contact. I take a deep breath, letting it fill my lungs, steady my pulse.

"This is it," I murmur. "Time to know."

I tap the screen.

"So you're ready," he says. No greetings. No small talk.

"How did you know?"

"James isn't the only one who knows everything, Asahi." his voice is warm, contrasting Mr. Wyatt's cool monotone. "So, are you ready?"

"It's Azrail," I correct. "And yes. I am."

It's time to know everything. I just hope I don't regret it.

About the Author

A.B. Monnette is a young author who grew up in Haiti before moving to the United States. Due to bullying and discrimination, Ms. Monnette did what she knew best. She read, daydreamed, and eventually started writing.

She discovered Wattpad at thirteen, which brought her into the world of opportunities and romance books. Eventually, the lack of black female protagonists left the hopelessly romantic out. Ms. Monnette decided that if she couldn't find her representation, she'd make her own.

Her first book, Only You, began as short stories she shared with her friend in their English class. Due to her mental illness, she took a break and did not get back to writing books until four years later, during the COVID-19 Quarantine.

Even though English is not her first language, A.B. Monnette kept writing and editing all of her books until they were as perfect as possible. With encouragement from family and friends, she decides to publish on Amazon.

Through her writing, readers can understand the mind of A.B. Monnette. A young woman whose dreams are incorporated into her writing.

When she's not writing, Ms. Monnette works on her master's degree, goes shopping and karaoke with friends, and daydreams about new stories.

Also by A.B Monnette

Love Me Trilogy

Touch Me

Heal Me - TBA

House of Suit Series

Tender Poison - Saving Oliver

Book 2 (Hearts) - Out 2026

Book 3 (Diamonds) - TBA

Book 4 (Clubs) - TBA